The Promises of Love

Roozan Aggarwal

First published in 2017 by
Becomeshakespeare.com

Wordit Content De sign & Editing Services Pvt Ltd
Unit - 26, Building A -1, Nr Wadala RTO,
Wadala (East), Mumbai 400037, India
T: +91 8080226699

Wordit Art Fund helps deserving authors publish their
work by providing monetary support. To apply for
funding, please visit us at
www.BecomeShakespeare.com

ISBN: 978-93-86487-78-0

Acknowledgement

I would like to thank my parents and my sister who have supported me throughout the journey of my life. They have been pillars to my upbringing and played an important role in shaping my success story.

I would also like to express my gratitude towards my friends who have been there to support me during my ups and downs of my life. They have played a crucial role in helping me to write this book.

Writing this book would not have been possible without constant support of my office colleagues. They have been my family away from my family. They have played an important role in my professional development and I can write essays for all the help that they have done during my term in office.

Contents

About The Author

Roozan Aggarwal writes books, which, considering where you're reading this, makes perfect sense. He's best known among his colleagues as the night walker, when he actually puts in nights to attain the corporate goals.

A strong believer to the fact that learning never stops. Thus even after graduating, putting hours in his startup and spending the little time left with him in his internship and further studies, he makes sure to try a different subject altogether on his lazy weekends.

To be a writer, you have to love books and be a book worm they say. It was never a case with him. In fact, in his initial years after school, he never touched novels thinking it to be bore. But it was this one train ride, where he purchased a novel out of the blue and from thereafter it changed his life.

Books to him are a key to his own world. A world where he doesn't live to anyone's expectations. A world where he has the authority to everything. A world where no one has any control over his thoughts.

He is also a dedicated gamer and never misses any chance of spending hours romancing in playstation and being a couch potato thereafter.

He can be reached on his mail id: Roozan.aggarwal@gmail.com

Prologue

The stage was set for the chief guest to arrive, the student audience already packed the entire auditorium and were waiting eagerly for the award ceremony to begin. It was an award ceremony at Chanakya School of Management Studies.

My name is Devang Shah and I am a business consultant. I was waiting too for my friend Siddhant Shergill to arrive at the venue.

Siddhant Shergill, a young business tycoon who had looks to die for. Fair complexion, tall height and short curly hairs. He was a heartthrob to women in and out of his business group. Gems magazine named him as the most eligible bachelor in 2016. But it wasn't only looks, Siddhant had brains of Einstein when it came to business. He started to crack complex business deals and strategic tie ups since initial stages in his business. Though coming from small town by the name of Haldwani- a marvelous city, which forms the gateway of Kumaon, I had never seen him struggling in dealing with senior level executives.

Yes! He was the chief guest of the award ceremony.

I have been working as his corporate consultant since 5 years and friend with him since last 2 years. During these 2 years, I insisted him many times for marrying someone but it all went in vain. There was something which bugged him whenever I tried to hook him up with someone.

He arrived at the venue on time; for him each and every minute was worth a price. A matte black BMW X6 arrived at the college gate. He didn't wait for chauffer or security to open the door for him. Though he is flying high in the skies of success but his feet are still cemented to the ground of humility.

He was wearing a black business suit donned with white shirt and red tie. As he stepped out of the car, he was escorted with his security to the auditorium. As he entered , the auditorium was filled with loud noises of applause and hooting which they did to express their affection and gratitude to their favorite alumni.

The award ceremony commenced with lamp lighting, a cultural dance and the brief agenda of the ceremony. This ceremony was done every year to award students with the best business ideas and it acted as a token of encouragement for them to perform better in the practical front.

Back in history of the college, Siddhant was a winner too and today the college witnessed him as the chief guest to the ceremony.

You all must be wondering what was I doing in that college even though I wasn't the alumni. The fact was Siddhant made sure that I accompany him like his shadow to meetings and ceremonies. I used to make sure that everything functioning fine to ensure minimum wastage of his time.

The main event began where top teams selected by jury were presenting their ideas for one last time to the audience. The ideas presented were great and in line with need of today's requirement of dynamic surroundings.

After an hour of proposing the business ideas, it was time to announce the winner and Siddhant was called to give away the award to the winner.

Siddhant was given the card which had the name of the winner and there was a stark change in his expressions. His eyebrows frowned and fingers began to tremble. His head started to sweat and his eyes were looking out for someone in the audience. I had never seen him trembling and sweating unless it was scorching heat.

The winner was called upon stage. Her name was Shivyanka Tandon. A tall heighted fair girl with chubby face with neck length dark brown hair. She had a perfect smile on those pink lips and her teeth shone like pearls.

Siddhant immediately left the auditorium as soon as he gave the award and informed me to meet at his home after the event. Siddhant seemed to be disturbed of fact and I had no ideas whatsoever. In his absence, I was called upon the stage to give the closing speech.

The audience didn't seem to care much about my speech as all of them expected a handsome businessman giving the speech rather than one of his consultants.

Sometimes, it's not the words that matter but the people who say those words matter.

I reached his home and the door was already opened. Siddhant didn't lived in a fancy penthouse or a bungalow. He had a one-bedroom flat in a descent society. The door was already open and Siddhant was sitting on the sofa as I entered.

His head hung low and he was still in his suit. 'Make me a drink he said' I went towards the kitchen he had and made him a drink the way he liked.

He was standing in the balcony staring and said with sorrow that 'her name was Shivyanka'.

It was the first time when I heard him talking about some girl. He made me sit on one of the bean bags while he sat on the other and began to recite a story.

A story which I had no idea about. It was the story of his life, how the most eligible bachelor is single and not looking for any girl. I was about to hear and see the secret side of Siddhant.

CHAPTER 1

The Beginning

It was just another day of my class in school. I used to be in third class and was just another back bencher who never focused on studies. I remember, I got a punishment in the first period itself that day and was standing outside the class.

Other students passing by were staring at me while I gave them my angry look just when I saw a girl whom I never saw in school before.

She had two ponies tied up in red ribbon and a pink bag with Disney princesses on it. She hopped like a bunny while holding her dad's finger. His father was in a navy uniform and had a furious look on his face.

He had thick black mustache and short hair which were too difficult to notice in the uniform cap that he wore. The honor of being in navy clearly reflected over his face.

His father's aura was so charming and glorious that I didn't notice how she looked.

They went straight inside my class without even noticing me standing there as if I was nothing to them.

I guess people staring at me during punishments made it habitual for me being noticed.

Her father came out after sometime leaving her in class and went out of the sight soon. I realized she was a new student in our school.

The class got over and I was called back in. I saw her sitting near the window staring at the ground outside. Guess she was hoping for someone in her family to pick her up from school.

I didn't notice much about her and went straight to my desk. Lessons after lessons the day passed until the last period got over and we packed our bags to head to our home sweet home.

The next day I arrived bit early and saw her sitting in the class. She was the first one to arrive followed by me. She looked at me for a moment and waved her hand. I waved back and sat on my desk.

She came to my desk and asked my name. 'Siddhant Shergill' I said in haste. Being a back bencher, other classmates never preferred talking to me. It was a first time when someone was talking to me without me taking pains to initiate a convo.

'Can I have a notebook of yours? I have to complete the pending work. I am Shivyanka Juneja and I am new here' she said. I was at that point of convo where I was staring at her like a creep.

She had blue eyes and was had a fair complexion. She had a cute nose and the two ponies only added icing on the cake.

'Sure, I can give you my English notebook after the school gets over' I said. She thanked me and went back to her desk. The day passed and we had frequent eye contacts during the class.

After the end of last period, she came to my desk and asked for the notebook. I gave her the notebook. She gave me a toffee in return.

She said that she used to carry toffees in school which she used to have if she ever felt annoyed or had bad mood.

The next day, she was bit late and came to my desk after the first lesson to return my notebook.

'Thanks for the help' she said. I guess it was the first time in my life when I was thanked for something. I was only punished in one way or the other.

I believe she found the traits of a good and helpful boy in the body of a back bencher.

It was a games period when I noticed her playing with few puppies in the school ground. I went to her and asked if I could play with her too.

'Sure, I love puppies'. Well those were the things which always scared the shit of out of me. But still to play with the only friend I had then, I would be ready to do anything.

She was cuddling them and sometimes also kissing them on the nose. She opened her hair bun and kept the hair band on the ground. When one of the puppies ran away with it. She started to cry and I knew nothing I could do then.

The best I knew then was to run to catch that puppy and try snatching the rubber band from him.

He made me run in the whole school ground which included water puddles, mini nursery and piles of mud which was being used for further construction work.

By the time I got the rubber band back to her, my uniform was filled with dirt all over. Also I had scratched one of my knee while chasing. 'Thanks' she said. All the pain seemed to go away the way she said it.

I was taken to the first aid room and dressing was done. Next I was taken to principal's office where my parents were called. They thought I was involved in another mischievous activity which lead to all of this.

My mom came to discuss the things with the principal and I was sent back home with her that day. On reaching home, my mom got angry due to this behavior. I didn't know what to say to her then.

I couldn't tell the truth that I was involved in some puppy issue because she knew that that's the last thing I would play with. However, my dad was so bottled up with my school complaints that it didn't matter to him anymore.

The next day she came up to my desk during the lunch with a sorry card and also her mother made a cupcake which she passed onto me as a gesture of thanks to get her that hair band.

'Sorry, I didn't know what to say then when they took you to principal's office.' she said. I said her that it was nothing new for me and I am at least called once in a week to the office.

'Friends?' she said. I waited to hear this since day one. 'Definitely' I said.

She was my first friend in the school who knew the real me in the body of an irresponsible guy.

*****

'Are you serious boss! How can you be one of those back benchers? You have topped in your management school' I asked.

'Devang! you just can't decide somebody's destiny based upon his class performance.' Siddhant said.

Siddhant completed his drink and went to change. In the meanwhile, I ordered a pizza from Domino's. I knew it was going to be a long night. I wanted to know what happened next.

I got a text from my girlfriend Avni, who reminded me for our dinner date that night which completely went of my mind that night. I wanted to go out with her as I had been busy with my office work lately and she was looking forward to meet me that night. But it's not always when you would hear a business tycoon telling you about his love life.

I called her up and explained the reason as to why I couldn't join her for the date. She did get annoyed but I do know that she understands me and deep down under she knew that Siddhant needed me more than her at the moment.

I didn't realize when Siddhant came back to the balcony after changing and heard me talking over the phone.

'You should go out with Avni, see you in office tomorrow' said Siddhant. He had a guilt on his face of holding me to hear his personal life.

'No! I think you need me more than her. She will understand. Also, I will take off tomorrow and take her to a road trip' I said. ' Sure, get it reimbursed too. My treat' laughed Siddhant.

'So what happened next?' I asked with interest. I wanted to know more and more of this mystery man. In our two years of friendship, I never saw his emotional side.

He had words locked in his heart which needed a key to open. I guess the girl's name in the award ceremony was the key to this lock.

'Let me get beer bottles first' Siddhant said.

I arranged the glasses while Siddhant took out the beer from the chiller.

The bottles were popped open, the glasses were filled and so was Siddhant's heart and my phone with Avni's text describing how lucky she was to have me in her life.

*****

CHAPTER 2

The Birthday Party

It was near end of class 4th when I was invited for her birthday party. During these two years we had grown out to be close friends with each other. She helped me with my studies wherever she could. Seeing my grades improve, teacher made us sit together. Our parents used to interact with each other in the parent teacher meetings and they didn't had enough words to thank their daughter for helping me out with my studies.

Though the parents interacted with each other, but I never had chance to visit her place before. I dressed in my best that day. I made her a birthday card which had all the stickers and smileys and colorful cake in which colors were outside the margins. I had no interest in drawing back then and it was the best I could do.

My mom got her a pink teddy bear which also played birthday jingles when its nose was pressed. My mom was invited too but she had some relatives coming that day so I had to go alone. Her dad sent a car to pick me up from my place.

It was a sedan which I used to see only on posters. I didn't know the car brands back then but I don't think it was nothing less than a Honda or Toyota. The chauffer was wearing a white uniform and he opened the door for me. I wasn't used to this rather I couldn't ask my dad to do this.

I sat in the car and found it was the luxurious car I witnessed in my life then. It had company fitted disc player and a trendy looking speedometer. My stomach was filled with butterflies and excitement was in my mind during the journey seeing other people checking me out in the car. They might have thought it was my car but that was clearly something my dad couldn't afford.

I reached her home after an hour long exciting car drive. It was a bungalow located at one of the prime locations of the city. The entry gate looked magnificent. It was a big black painted iron gate which had two security man guarding it all the time. The gates were opened upon seeing the car followed by the salute.

I knew it was going to be the most happening day for me. It had a big porch on which the car stopped. I headed inside the home. The house had a tall ceiling on which hanged a chandelier which seemed to be made of crystal. I didn't know what crystal was back then. I thought anything made out of diamond looking glass is supposed to be crystal.

The floor had white marble which was brighter than the teeth's of model shown in toothpaste advertisement.

'You must be Siddhant I believe' said a heavy voice as I was staring at the flooring. I turned back and saw a man standing in black formals with a dark grey tie. He was Shivyanka's father. I greeted him, touched his feet and he shook my hand. It was a tight grip. Guess, all the defense personnel are habitual of a firm handshake.

He escorted me to the garden where the party took place. I knew it's again going to be a big garden which might had a swimming pool. My guess wasn't wrong when I saw the garden. It was a big garden which was filled with the children playing on the bouncy and parents and navy officials interacting with each other.

Most of them seemed to be part of high class societies who had a fake smile all the time on their faces. I saw Shivyanka waving at me from the bouncy asking me to join her.

She was wearing a pink fairy dress and the hair were curled to complement the fairy look. She had pink gloves along with it. She actually looked like a little fairy, a cute bubbly fairy rather.

We bounced and played on the bouncy. She threw balls on me and asked me to do the same in return. I couldn't hit her though as she looked lovely. Had I been judge of any cute looking child awards, I would have given her the award without any nomination procedure.

She was called by her father to cut the cake. She grabbed my hand and took me along with her. It was a big strawberry cake which had her edible photographs on it. The cake was cut and she I got the first bite of it followed by her parents.

Soon after eating the cake and snacks she took me inside her home to show her room. She had a big room which had all kinds of toys. My gift clearly didn't make a place there.

'What did you get me' she asked me with possessiveness. 'Definitely not something which you don't have' I replied.

'Show me please' she requested. I went to the gifts table to collect my card and the gift I got for her and went back to her room. She put the gift aside and read the card I made for her.

She liked it so much that she taped the same on the wall.

'It's one of the best gifts I had today!' she exclaimed with joy and hugged me. No one ever hugged me before. But it seriously made me happy when I realized that my hard work on the card did render me result in the end.

That proved to be the best day for me. My parents witnessed the level of happiness when after reaching the home, I rushed into my room and hid under the blanket. My face flushed red and cheeks looked like strawberry ice cream scoops.

From that day onwards, my parents started to tease me by taking her name and I used to hide myself due to shyness. The classes seemed to be lovely and I used to sit with her everyday.

Once, teacher made a girl sit between us and we used to tease her a lot that she had to change her seat. The friendship grew stronger day by day.

*****

The door-bell buzzed and the story telling session was interrupted. 'I thought I had no appointments. How can people disturb someone at this hour?' asked Siddhant. I forgot to tell him before that I ordered a pizza. Guess this is what happens when you hear a great story that you tend to forget things.

'I think it's the pizza guy. I forgot to tell you that I ordered some.' I reverted. I opened the door and as expected a man in the blue uniform was waiting for us with a fake smile on his face holding big pizza bag on one of his palms.

I paid the amount and collected pizzas and coke from him. 'Why do we need coke when we have beers with us?' asked Siddhant. 'Are you going to stop only on beers tonight? I thought we might end up having some rum and whiskey' I said with a wicked smile.

Siddhant went to kitchen to take his favorite chili sauce while I took the pizzas out of the box and served them on the plate.

'If you think that I am being a bore, you can watch football match. It's FIFA final after all.' Siddhant said. 'Yes Sid, it's the most boring night of my life, now let's not waste time these pizzas want to get eaten soon' adding humour.

The pizzas looked tempting. These were chicken pizzas with cheese burst base and cheese is my weakness. Without further ado I grabbed my first bite, the piping hot cheese burnt my mouth.

'Easy my boy' Siddhant exclaimed. I looked him with the bunny eyes as he wiped the cheese from my face with the napkin.

'So it was your first luxurious car ride?' I asked with curiosity. 'Yes absolutely, my dad owned a Maruti and it wasn't even close to what her father owned' Siddhant replied.

'So what happened next? You guys started dating' I joked

'Well Devang, things don't end always in the manner that you want them to be. You got to adapt yourself to the unexpected situation that life throws at you time and again' Siddhant told. I was wondering what did it meant while he continued his story.

*****

CHAPTER 3

The Big News

It was usual scenario when me and Shivyanka used to talk with each other over calls after school hours. We used to discuss about cartoons, homework and what not. Once, we discussed on how she planned to run away from home if her mother made green vegetables for one more time.

Anyway, the result of class 4th were declared and I managed to pass while Shivyanka topped the class. Sometimes, I believed that it was Shivyanka's hard work that I managed to pass. She used to make sure that I used to sit with her during classes and focus on studies rather than fooling around with other boys.

We used to call each other throughout the day. Sometimes, our mom's used to take us to the other's house to play rather than talking over the call.

Her mom invited us for lunch once. Her mom prepared variety of food items ranging from soups, rice, curry, dal to jelly, kheer and cake. Her mom was one of the best cooks, though not better than my mom. Well this is what I used to say to my mom.

It was a wonderful feast and I was delighted by the hospitality her mom offered us with. I remember that we were having ice cream and watching cartoon in her bedroom when she came to me and said that she would be changing school for class 5th.

For a minute it didn't register in my mind. For the second minute, I got my shit together to ask her again 'Are you serious'. I didn't know back then that we were allowed to leave school after completing a class. Moreover, I just couldn't imagine myself without her. All the memories seemed to flash in front of my eyes, from the day we first met till date.

'Yes, dad thinks that it will be better for my future' she said with sorrow. She didn't seem to be happy either. Out of all the students in the class, she chose to be my friend when she joined. There was definitely a connection between us which helped in creating a strong bond of friendship between us.

'You can join too; we will sit together in the new school too' she suggested. But I knew that just couldn't be possible. Changing school wasn't an easy task specially when your father doesn't earn well. She was too immature to understand this.

I rushed to my mom who was having tea with her mom in the garden and told her the story. Mom said that she knew it way before when her parents were initially deciding to switch the school. I guess I was the last one to be informed about her decision.

'So what? You can come to play with her whenever you want' her mom said consoling me. But I just didn't want to play with her. I wanted to study with her in the class, have lunch together and also play with puppies in the school ground. But I just couldn't say this to them.

I ran back to her room where she was still watching the television. 'I will miss you, don't forget me' I said. 'On one condition, that you will study hard in class and stay away from all the nuisance in school.' She said.

I promised her that I would turn out to be one of the top scorers from class 5th and would take time to meet her as and when it would be feasible.

With a heavy heart I left her home, carrying thousands of memories of her in my heart I waved her bye for the one last time. I knew even if thousands of promises were made to stay connected the things wouldn't turn out to be normal as before.

We headed back to our home, the excitement for new academic session was already drained enough to make me depressed. Things weren't going to be same without her again.

Not a single day during the vacation had passed where I didn't call her asking how she was and what was the status of her new school. I kind of forgot myself during this time. She made a place in my mind then.

Soon, it was the first day of class 5th. Like every other kid, I was given a new bag and new set of stationary. The pleasing smell of new books filled the entire classroom. However, the eyes were looking for something else in the class. They were searching for Shivyanka, there was a little hope that she would turn up on the first day.

But I had to bear the fact that she would not be coming now. She left the school and she would be sitting somewhere in her new school with new set of classmates. For once I wanted to cry and rush back home. I didn't want to study in the class where she was not present but every time when I had this thought my mind would trigger with the promise I made to her.

To stand by the promise I made, I requested the teacher to make me sit with the topper of the class. His name was Karan. A tall heighted wheatish complexioned guy who wore rimless specs. He was the most intelligent guy I knew after Shivyanka.

Karan and I never talked with each other during the past years of the school life. I didn't know his nature, his way of working or his methodology of thinking and responding to situations. But to keep up with the promise I made to Shivyanka, I had to take a risk which was worth giving a try.

I didn't have any expectations from him in the beginning. I thought I was all alone without Shivyanka being on my side but situation was completely different. Karan and I gelled up well. He used to help me with my math concept wherever I got stuck. The science seemed to be interesting the way he used to explain the fundamentals of elements and compounds to me. The history of roman and Indus Valley civilization wasn't bore too since Karan had his own method of memorizing the important developments in these civilizations.

On the other hand, my talks with Shivyanka gradually decreased over the period of time. We got focused towards studies. We had our own set of goals which we needed to achieve to be toppers of our classes.

The honeymoon period was over after the first month itself and we had unit tests followed by mid -term assessment and ending up with final examinations. The effect of being in good company now began to reflect in my grades. I performed well in the unit tests and scored the third position in the class during the mid-term assessment.

However, after the mid -term Karan had to leave the school due to his dad's transfer abroad. I was back to square one being all alone. Also there was a bigger problem now, I had to justify my scores in the next set of assessments. I didn't want others to think it as a fluke. It was then I decided if I have to be best I have to do it my way then rather than using someone else's method of scoring the marks.

Every day after school, I used to sit in library and make notes from all the relevant reference books available. I used to reach home by evening and memorize those notes before sleeping. The mornings used to start early where I would make a list of subjects which were to be studied that day in the library.

Yes, when I got serious towards studies, I stopped talking to Shivyanka. It wasn't the fact that I didn't want to rather I had no time to do so. In fact, she didn't call up either. I had no idea as to if she was even in the city or not.

The time for final examinations arrived when we got our date sheets. Every one back then used to get scared seeing the date sheet and would cut their contact from the outside world from that day itself.

I on the other hand started to prepare way before so I was least concerned and scared. The exams began as per the dates in the date sheet. I used to sleep early before the exam day and used to wake up early morning for final round of revisions. My father used to drop me to school and used to collect me up after the exam got over.

Sometimes, I still wonder if he went home during the exam hours.?

The final assessments got over and soon we had the result day. I prayed a thousand times that day not just for the marks but for the success towards this new life I was heading too.

A life where I would not be dependent on some other student for one thing or the other. A life where I would have control over myself and I would know what's right for me and what not. Today was the transition day of a back bencher to a serious studious guy.

I headed to school with high hopes but little did I know about the consequences of what would happen when the marks would be shown.

I had expectations to score second or third position at most but who knew life had different plans for me. I topped the class with flying colors. Classmates clearly witnessed transformation of slacky backbencher to a class topper.

It is implied that my parents were happy and they had tears of joy when they checked my score card. Again my hard work paid off. I wasn't a back bencher now; I was a hard working class topper.

*****

'So this is how you changed?' I questioned Siddhant. 'Yes, exactly. See I wasn't a topper since childhood. Things changed once Shivyanka left me' I guess Siddhant couldn't describe it better.

'So what happened next? You started talking with her again?' my curiosity increased with each passing phase in Siddhant's childhood. He truly proved to be a mystery man. He had so much to share still he never did.

He needed someone to listen to, someone whom he can count on. In these today's fast moving business life, a person can't trust other one. You never know how people may play with your emotions.

'By the way, we finished the whiskey already. Want to try something else?' Siddhant asked. 'The story is creating a mood of its own. We will try something else later' I answered.

'Okay, so this is what happened next' Siddhant continued the story.

*****

Chapter 4

The New School-Part 1

'It wasn't the only good news that ringed our ears that week. My father got promoted and became branch manager too' he exclaimed. The best thing about government job's promotion is it is not only a promotion but also a source of freebies like a car, bigger home, a servant and better family travel bonuses.

That week became a festive week for us since I was the first to top in any class among my other family members and my dad got a long due promotion which he truly deserved. But soon we had to face a harsh reality. We had to leave the house since we were now allotted with a bigger one and I also had to change my school since the new place was really far from my school.

I never valued that house. It had oily kitchen tiles, drawing and markings on the wall and dirty garage filled up with mud and dirt and smelled of Greece. However, this act of moving into a new place made me think differently.

This wasn't just a house for me, it was a home. A place, where the markings on the walls were the witness of my growth and the drawings were proof of my creativity. The marks of oil on the kitchen tiles were a proof of my mom's delicious cooking. The dirt marks in the garage reflected my dad's love for his car which he used to wash every weekend.

I was born there, and it had become a part of my life. It gave my family a roof and now it was left for other Siddhant to be grown and enjoy his childhood in that happy place.

The final day came when we left that house. We had a taxi which took us to this new place. This new place looked very similar to the locality where Shivyanka lived. I didn't know the exact directions to her place because I was busy noticing the features of her car then.

But one thing I surely remember was a palatial school which crossed my way both the times i.e., when I was going for her party and when I was moving to my new home.

Further after a ten minutes' drive, the car stopped outside a big bungalow. This is what I was supposed to call a 'home' now.

It also resembled somewhat like her house. It had a big black gate which was guarded by a security guard. It had a small porch where a new car waited for my dad to drive. It was a luxurious Hyundai Sedan which was recently launched in the market. It had a big garden which was populated with all kinds of flowers one could imagine at a given point of time.

Dad took out keys from his pocket and opened the door. The door opened with a fishy sound, guess it was reflection of some other Siddhant's work who used to live there before we moved. The house opened to a drawing room which had flooring of a shining white marble and a designer paint on the walls.

It also had a comfortable sofa set which was angled perfectly with a big flat screen television mounted on the wall. It looked exactly what one gets to see in the advertisement wishing to buy one.

Moving further, it had set of three large size air conditioned bedrooms with nice furniture and wooden flooring. Back then air conditioners and flat screen televisions were signs of luxury and status rather than necessity.

My mom went to the place where she loved spending time i.e., kitchen followed by me. It was a modular kitchen with chimney and stuff. I didn't know any of those equipment back then but she seemed to definitely had idea of all that technical stuff.

It took us whole day to one bedroom when we all of us slept on one bed. The next morning was different from the mornings that I used to experience in my previous home. Instead of car's traffic, I could hear bird's cooing and dusty sky seemed to had been replaced by blue one's. I felt lucky that day to have moved up in my life and experience things which many of people would dream for.

I was still in bed when I could hear dad talking on his cellphone and packing his things up. I could see a completely different person in him that day. He wore a perfect business suit instead of regular shirt and trouser and he now carried a laptop bad.

I wonder where was it all the time. He took his new car keys and drove off. The engine sounded like honey to the ears. It was cars which excited me rather than some cartoons and stuff back then.

Going back inside the house I was helping my mom when the doorbell ringed. I opened the gate and I saw a well-built man having big black moustache who was is his early thirties and had a scar on his face. He seemed to be scary, I ran back inside crying. I thought he was a goon.

My mom seeing me crying, went to check who he was. A few minutes later, she came inside along with him and told me that he was a full time servant who was appointed by dad's company. His name was Shyamak and he headed from a town by the name of Kalinga in Haryana.

He also told that his father was a farmer and he came to city in search of work. All of this info didn't make him look scary any longer.

My mom explained him the work while I watched my favorite set of movies on the television. Well I guess you got to enjoy this honeymoon period.

The dad arrived early that night and we sat on the dining table for dinner. Generally, my mom used to cook while we wait for it in the dining room but now thanks to Shyamak the whole family sat together while he prepared the food.

Coming to the taste of food, he was a great cook. Though he didn't know fancy dishes like my mom did, but all that he made tasted delicious. The curry rice prepared by him were my favorite.

The next few days went quite relaxed until one day I was told that I had to prepare for an entrance examination for class 6$^{th.}$ How could I forget that I had to study? The honeymoon period seemed to be over now and I was back in the study mode. If this was enough, I was informed about this just a day before exam.

I studied and checked the net on whatever study material I could get my hands on and started to mug and cram the things up. Understanding and learning the concepts would take time which I was short of. I studied till late night and didn't realize as to when I fell asleep. I remember next day being awaken by my mom. I could hear her shouting that I would get late if I didn't get ready. I had no time to bath even.

I washed my face with soap and oiled my hair. I sat on the back seat of the car while mom sat on the front. Shyamak prepared breakfast and packed in a box for me. It was the first time when I sat in dad's new car. It looked better than what Shivyanka's car looked like. It had a screen on the music system which showed route to places I can visit and other unique feature it had was I could see things behind my car if my car was in reverse mode.

My dad informed me that it was called 'Navigation system and reverse parking camera'. Dad turned on the engine and took the car out of the house. The house guard saluted him. This was something which I would take time to get comforted with.

Dad punched 'Green Valley School' in the navigation system and system directed the route towards the destination. I didn't know which school it was since I was hearing the name for the first time. The route resembled to some place which I couldn't recall.

After a few minutes' drive, I could see that palatial school again and dad slowed his car as he came across the parking bay. Mom and me got off the car while dad took it towards the parking. After ten minutes, dad came back and took us inside the school.

The school was very well guarded by set of guards guarding the main entrance gate, who won't allow anyone to enter without a valid identity card. My dad informed about his appointment with the principal and showed the confirmation letter to the head guard for the same.

The head after looking at the letter and confirming it over the phone, permitted us to enter the premises.

My first impression seeing the school was 'What the fuck'. This school was as big as a city in itself and my previous school stood nowhere close to this one. It had a big ground where one could witness all kinds of sporting activities ranging from cricket to horse riding.

My earlier school was smaller than the ground itself. Forget about horse riding, it didn't have proper gears for cricket either. Moving further was the admin block of the school where one could check the fees accounts and other related activities.

Principal was supposed to sit in this block. Dad asked for the directions from a peon to the principal's office and we headed towards the said direction.

Principal's office had its own charm. It had a nice coffee brown wooden furniture along with a couch where one could comfortably sleep on. An aquarium in the corner which had a pair of gold fish in it.

The principal's room had everything from television to fridge but it lacked one important thing i.e., principal herself. Yes, she wasn't there but we had no other option than to wait for her and we waited for her like an hour.

My dad frequently checked his watch to check the time. Guess he had an urgent meeting to attend. Just as we decided to leave and headed towards the office gate, came a lady rushing towards us. She was the principal Ms. Rohini Shah.

She was a fair lady in her late forties. She had a neck length hair and wore rimless spectacles. She was wearing a saree with a sleeveless blouse that day. The stress she took to maintain the decorum and the experience was easily reflected through the stretch lines on forehead and her white hair.

She requested us to sit back again and apologized for being late, she was stuck in teacher's meeting. She sat on her chair and massaged her forehead while she went through my grades.

I remember that she asked the reason for the poor grades and then further significant improvement which made me stood first in the class.

I answered her that it was due to a promise which I made to a friend who was leaving that school. A promise which was so strong that made me realize my actual potential and encouraged me to give my best. I also assured her that if I get selected for admission, I would give my best towards studies and get laurels for school in the future.

Guess, it was this speech which made her skip my written test round and selecting me later that day after oral tests of vocabulary.

I still had a week to join and had nothing in my hand to do apart from buying books, stationary and uniform. Mom and me used to leave for the market in the morning and get back by afternoon for the purchases. After that, it used to be a love affair between me and television where I used to watch all kinds of movies aired for the rest of the day.

In the meanwhile, during these days of being idle, I asked Shyamak for help. He knew the area well therefore, I requested him if he could help me finding out Shivyanka's house. I gave him the description of the house and what her dad did, only if it was of some help.

I used to look at Shyamak's face daily waiting for him to give me a good news that he has found the address and she misses me too but Shyamak's expressionless face gave all the answers to my queries.

It was last day of that so called vacation when Shyamak approached me to give the news that the house was few blocks away. Hearing this news, I was so happy that I completely lost the track of what he said next. What followed it was definitely not a good news, that they had to a new house and he didn't have any idea where this new house was.

It gave me some serious mood crush and I switched off the television and went back to my room sobbing. Mom asked what the reason was when entered the room with sandwich that Shyamak made for me to cheer the mood up.

I said it was nothing but the thought that I would be missing the flat screen television during the school hours. Guess, it was the first time when I lied to my mom.

Well after the dinner that day, I was standing in the balcony when Shyamak approached me and asked what the deal was. Who was this girl and why was I looking for her? I told him the entire scenario starting from the punishment where I first saw her till the time when I finally parted from her. Yes, it did include her car description which I surely loved.

I didn't realize how the time flied reciting the story when Shyamak interrupted me and informed the time. It was twelve already and the school was supposed to start in next seven hours. I seriously didn't want to be late on day one.

CHAPTER 5

The New School-Part 2

It was half past five when my dad woke me up. I was awoken from a deep sleep where I was dreaming of winning car race in Formula one. Never mind, so I got ready for school which used to take nearly an hour and then heading to the breakfast table.

The uniform was a crisp white shirt with a school logo of a shield on the pocket of the shirt and a red colored shorts with white and yellow colored checks on it.

Shyamak used to serve cornflakes in breakfast not because he wanted me to have it but because that's what my mom had instructed him to do. I gulped most of it rather than chewing for that particular set of minutes and rushed to dad's car.

Though I was provided with a school bus, but I wanted to ride in dad's car on the first day of the school. It was quarter to seven already when dad turned the engine on and he rushed the car towards the school.

It seemed all like that F1 dream again apart from the fact that the roads, the driver and the car was different but the speed was nearly same.

Only, five minutes were left for the school to start when dad dropped me on the gate and asked the security guard to escort me towards my class since I was new.

I passed through that big school ground again followed by admin block and reached the academic block after that. Academic block was a 5 floored white building which had around 80 centrally air conditioned classrooms, 10 labs and few empty store rooms. As informed by guard around four thousand students were studying in the school making it to be the biggest school in the city.

The junior classes were on the first floor and intermediate classes were on the second. Climbing the stairs for those two floors was a task. The class was located on the corner most part of the building and I was already sweating by the time guard took me there.

He left me there at the gate and I had a set of fifty students staring right at me. I was feeling butterflies in my stomach all this time and adjusting in a new school was not an easy task.

I found an empty seat in the very first row and sat on it. Children still looked at me as if they had seen an alien walking in their class.

A student came to me and introduced himself to be Sarthak Kataria. He had small eyes, short hair, short height and wore rectangular specs. He shook my hand and took me to his seat. I sensed something fishy in him initially but then thought it to be out of nervousness.

He started talking to me and I just couldn't get a word he was saying. Before I could do or figure anything out, he pushed me down to his seat and my ass got poked by the board pin. It hurt badly and I started to cry.

Teacher came soon after that and noticed me crying. She asked what the reason was and I said that I was just missing my parents. I noticed the look Sarthak had on his face. He struggled to figure out why I didn't complain about him. I had some better plans for his betterment, I didn't want it to end it in a normal way.

I was introduced with other students in the class and was told that a girl by the name of Shivyanka was on leave for a week. All the students belonged from more or less same kind of family background i.e., business It didn't took me a moment extra to realize that I was in a school where majority students belonged from elite class of the society.

The classes started after the introduction session and my honeymoon period was finally over. All I had now was a series of hectic class schedules and exams approaching towards me as days progressed towards the first week in school.

By the way, I forgot to tell the most important thing which happened on the first day. I was standing in the corridor after lunch when I felt a pat on my back. It was not a pat, rather it felt like a slap on the back. I turned back and saw my cousin standing.

His name was Rakul Mehta and he was my cousin from maternal side. Even though we lived in same city but we met only during marriages and other social gathering. His dad owned a mill outside the city which proved well as to how he was in the same school. He in fact was in the same grade but in different section.

We were having random conversations about cars when the bill for the next lesson ringed and I rushed back to my class.

I thought Rakul was just a normal cousin whom I would meet for once or twice in the school during a year and sometimes in the marriage.

But I seriously didn't have any idea as to what he can do to make my life hell in the future. Well that's why we say future is unpredictable.

*****

'What did he do exactly?' I asked.

He showed his hand and signaled me to wait.

'By the way, is it the same Sarthak Kataria, who is working as a clerk in Finance department? I believe he is from same school' I questioned. I have known Sarthak for quite a time now. His cubicle was right outside my cabin and I have always seen him in frustration.

'You got it. Bullseye!' Siddhant said with wicked smile on his face. 'So what was the revenge after all and why didn't you complain back then?' I added.

'Well, I seriously don't have the answer for the second and I want you to answer the first' said Siddhant.

It was one in the morning already and Siddhant gave me a task to find out the revenge. I accessed Siddhant's laptop to check his employee file. It took me couple of minutes to understand the entire situation and everything was now connecting with each other.

'I got it. After you gained control over the company, you hired Sarthak using your influences in the business world. Also, it is evident from his employee file that you didn't take the interview. Rather you couldn't take the interview because the designation was so low that an assistant manager could take it. Also, he is a referral employee, but the employee who has referred him is marked as confidential which proves the fact that it was your final decision to choose him in the company. His salary is four times more than the industry average and his designation is quite low than what he deserves.

He has been paid highly so that the luxury becomes his necessity and if he thinks to change the company, no other company would hire him at such high salary. So not promoting the deserved and also not letting him leave the company is the sweet revenge that you took' I was almost out of breath when I finished.

Siddhant looked with an amazed expression on his face.

'You are a rascal Siddhant' I said.

'You always prove that decision to hire you as my consultant was correct.' Said Siddhant poking his finger on my shoulder.

'What happened next' I was so intrigued to know the rest of the story.

Siddhant went to the washroom and came back after washing his face. He drank a glass of water and started recite the other part.

*****

CHAPTER 6

The Reunion

The first week in school went well. I was piled up with homework, sample test papers and tones of pending work which was already done before I joined the school.

If this was not enough, I had to choose a sport which I had to play throughout the year after school hours to excel in that particular sport. Playing cricket didn't seem to be tiring before and added to it was the heavy gear which we had to wear while playing it.

The weekend was better. Shyamak learnt to make pasta and it tasted wonderful. Shyamak did know the art of cooking and he was actually killing it.

Dad got me set of DVD's to watch on the television since, I used to get bore watching the same old set of movies which were frequently aired on television.

The weekend went well and I was ready for the next one. I reached the school well in time and saw a new girl sitting on the corner. I didn't see her face clearly since she had long hairs which covered her face while she read the book. Since, I was new I didn't prefer to talk to new faces specially after Sarthak's incident.

The other students started to pour in. I was waiting for the class teacher would introduce me to Shivyanka. Somewhere or the other, I wished her to be Shivyanka Juneja but what were the odds of that happening?

I took out a book and started to make notes when the teacher arrived. She saw Shivyanka and called her to my desk. Boy oh boy! She was Shivyanka Juneja, the Shivyanka Juneja my childhood friend.

I just couldn't get happier, she looked way better than what she looked few years back. Oh yes! The girl who was sitting in the corner when I entered the class was Shivyanka herself.

My smile met ear to ear and happiness of meeting her surely reflected over my face. But things changed soon, when she didn't reciprocate the same. It seemed she didn't recognize me and the hands we shook was pretty cold instead of a warm and hearty one.

She went back straight to her desk and started writing something on her notepad. I struggled to make out what just happened then while teacher started to diagrams on the board. She threw a chalk on me and asked why wasn't I writing. I still didn't write since I was so disturbed with this fact which lead to punishment where I stood outside the class.

It had been quite some time when I last got my punishment and that had a fun of its own. Anyway, I wasn't able to focus properly in class that day and went home without doing my cricket practice. On reaching home, the first thing I did was narrated the whole incident to mom who was shocked herself.

We had been good friends, and that was least expected from her. Later that night, I was studying in my room when Shyamak knocked the door and asked me if I was free. I let him in and made him sit on the other chair beside the study table.

He asked what the thing was which had spoilt my mood. I told her about how I met Shivyanka in school today and the way she reacted.

Shyamak suggested that maybe she had forgotten me and I just need to remind her. I thought it to be genuine since we guys didn't talk for a whole year and we had been busy in our own lives which generally revolved around studies. He did give some useful advices sometime.

The next day, I approached her in the morning when no one was around her and asked if she knew who I was. She nodded her head in negation and ordered me to get back to my desk or else she would complain if I bug her again.

Her voice was so loud that other children started to stare at me as if I was actually troubling her. I went back to my desk with head hung down in shame and sat down on the desk.

I made a strong mind that I would ignore her whatever the scenario will be and would focus only on my studies.

It was time around mid-terms and I had already proven myself earlier by topping the class in the unit tests which were conducted before mid-term assessments and Shivyanka was second. She treated me like her arch rival in class since I was the one who was being hindrance between her and top position in class. I also worked hard since I didn't want to come second either.

Somewhere deep down the heart, it all hurt me. The girl who helped me in being what I am today and who was my best friend once, took me for her enemy and was fighting against me for the top position. For once I wanted to leave all for her and be back to the way I was i.e. back bencher but the embarrassment acted like a motivational factor.

It was the exam time when each child was seen with a book all the time. It all resembled like a warfront, instead of weapons we had books where our eyes were glued all the time.

Back in home mom had instructed Shyamak to be attentive during nights just in case if I required something to eat or drink. Also, Shyamak used to bring me a warm glass of milk every midnight which helped me to concentrate.

Though my dad was a branch head now and had number of employees under him, still none of it affected his habit of dropping me school on exams days and waiting for me till the time I returned from the examination center.

The month long examination session ended and results were declared after a week's break. I again topped the class whereas Shivyanka stood third. I felt bad for her like really bad.

Things were going as planned for the next set of months and mom was now aware about my scene with her. She said that my decision of not talking with her was kind of straight forward and way too direct. I should have given her a chance but she surely didn't understand the embarrassment I had to face.

It was the month of December when were told about the final terms. However, before year end exams, projects were to be made on what had been taught in that particular year for all the subjects.

It was supposed to be done in pairs and out of all the children in class, teacher paired both of us. I didn't want to work with her but I had no other option.

Coming to the execution part, we chose library to work in since, it was the most silent place in school and it helped me to concentrate. We had formals talks between us which revolved around studies and project detailing. It was hard and painful for me at every step to avoid her.

One day while working on the project, I asked if she actually didn't know who I was or was it one of her pranks which she was playing on me. She apologized for her behavior and she said that she actually didn't know who I was though she studied in the same school.

It felt like thousand knives slitting my heart one after the other. But what she said next would cure half of them.

She said that though she didn't remember who I was but she won't mind to be my friend and start things from scratch. It was better than not talking to her at least. I forgot all the promises I made with myself and not talking to her in the beginning and immediately agreed to her proposal.

Sometimes, life and destiny have their own set of plans.

We talked, but still none of our talks had that set of comfort which existed earlier in the previous school. We had more to talk about studies and less of personal talks. Somehow we submitted the project on time and I realized I could have done better had the team been free from complications.

Just a week before the final examinations, the project marks were announced and ours was the best amongst all other sections of grade 6th. I was happy but still somewhere I wanted us to be normal again.

We had cricket try outs for school team during that week and coach had high endeavors from me. He wanted me to take as a spin bowler for the school cricket team. Coach was a bald man with thick black moustache and a mole on his cheek. Some children told that he played for few Ranji Trophy Championships but I had news of it.

The contenders for bowling in the cricket team comprised of students from class 5th to 8th. It felt as if I had no chances to make it to the final team. Each bowler was given six balls to bowl. The one on who's ball the batsmen make the lowest runs get to the team. Four bowlers were supposed to be chosen out of ten who were there for the trials that day.

I was the first one to be chosen for bowling trials. Shyamak once told to keep in mind during the trials that I had a control on my spins pretty well and it was just the coach who was made to be believed.

The coach handed over the ball to me. It was a season ball having scratches all over the shell. The person batting was the best batsman was the school team. I went for my first ball, I delivered an off spin which went for a straight drive, passing right beside my leg. Had I been a bit left, it would have definitely cracked my knee.

Then was the turn of second wall in which a leg spin helped me taking a wicket. A first wicket is always remembered and it was the best day of my life. The next batsman was Rakul, I had no ideas that he was in school team.

It was that moment when your parents brag all the time about your cousin's great performance and you wait for a moment to beat the shit out of them. It was that very moment, the token to that success was right in my hand it had only one hurdle to it.

I tried to deliver my best on spin to which Rakul played a defense. I was amazed. Rakul was actually a good batsman. The other ball was again played in a defense.

All my hopes to reach the door of success and beating the shit out of him seemed to be shattered. I had only one chance left and I knew I won't get this opportunity again.

While was taking a light run to deliver, my leg slipped right at the moment when I was throwing. I didn't know what that delivery was called but it definitely took a wicket. It was all by fluke but the look on face was something which was definitely which cannot be ignored. It felt as if somebody poked a cactus on his ass.

Six balls with two wickets was not a bad performance. The coach clapped while I returned back to the line-up of bowlers. The other bowlers were pretty well too. Some delivered maiden, some took a wicket, some even took three. The competition was tough since each bowler seemed to be better than the other.

But right after the try outs, results were announced and I made it to the team as spin bowler. It was the month of March and cricket matches were supposed to start from next month.

After the trials, I reached back to class and found that no one was there. I checked the scheduler and noticed that it was library lesson. I was already tired after the practice so therefore I decided to stay back and relax.

While I was resting with my head down on the table and eyes closed, I felt a hand on my hairs. The touch felt soft and lovely, it was so comforting that I wanted it to never end.

I looked up and found it to be Shivyanka's hand. Shivyanka was standing there and it seemed as if she wanted to say something.

I asked what happened. 'Did you top the class that year?' She asked. It took a minute for me to understand as to what had just happened.

She said that she was sorry to have completely forgotten me. Like all other girls, she did put on some blame to me that I should have continued calling her and shouldn't have boycotted her like that.

Well I just wanted to seize the moment rather than fighting who was the one to be blamed.

*****

'So how did she recalled the stuff if she had already forgotten everything about you?' I asked with curiosity.

'Want to think and give shot to it?' Siddhant reverted. Siddhant proposed to give me a task to think what made her remember about him. I seriously was not in a mood to do anymore thinking. I turned down the proposal and requested him to break the ice.

'Well how about a coffee before that?' Siddhant asked. It was half past two and none of us wanted to have any more alcohol. In fact, coffee was perfect for that very moment.

Siddhant went to the kitchen and I followed him. It wasn't a very big modular kitchen and all that blingy stuff wasn't there. It was a simple kitchen which had all the basic necessities which a common man would require in his daily life.

He took the coffee bottle out of the cupboard while I warmed the milk over the gas stove. He filled coffee in the mugs and poured the milk in those mugs. I arranged some snacks since my hunger stroke back.

We went back to the balcony and the weather was pretty pleasant. The cold winds touched our face as we sipped hot coffee. I bit a biscuit and asked the same question again.

'See Devang, I hope you remember I made a card for her on her birthday' Siddhant asked. I nodded and confirmed it.

'So, she shifted her house a few blocks away. At the time of shifting, her family kept the card in some cargo box while moving. Later on in the new house, Shivyanka couldn't find the card when she was arranging her room. Her mom didn't know about it either so she made an excuse that it was lost somewhere in the transit. The card and my phone calls was the only connection we had. Over the period of time both of these were eliminated hence, she wasn't able to recall me. After meeting her again in new school and behaving awkwardly with her, she looked her class photo albums to look for me and it was then she found the birthday card in one of those boxes' Siddhant explained.

'You seemed to be a pretty nice artist. A card so good that she actually forgot you when she lost it' I joked.

*****

CHAPTER 7

The Split And The Innings

My feelings sky rocketed when we started to talk again and things sorted between us. No doubt, the exams went fine too for both of us. I topped the class again and she stood second. But she wasn't angry or annoyed by this. Rather, she was happy that I was still living my promise that I once made with her.

The session break was a month long break where we were supposed to rest and gear up for the next academic year. But due to my regular cricket practice for upcoming tournament, resting was something which I used to rarely do.

My dad used to drop me and Shyamak every day to the school for my cricket practice. Shyamak used to stay in the school canteen during the practice and used to take me home after practice hours. He made sure that I don't have junk food available in school canteen. Sometimes, he was more of my parent's detective rather than the caretaker of our house.

Due to regular practice sessions I didn't realize when the session break got over and I had to join school back again.

It was the first day for class 7th. The classes moved a floor higher, due to regular cricket practice, climbing these floors wasn't a task anymore.

I went to the section designated and noticed that all the sections were reshuffled. In fact, most of the friends from class 6th were nowhere to be seen and did included Shivyanka. Her section was different too. We had to sit in the sections allotted since these were all approved by the principal. I went inside and sat on an empty desk in the middle row.

I generally preferred sitting on the first row but all the seats in the front row were occupied with toppers from other sections. I didn't require a front row to top my class, I would do that sitting on the last row too, this was the level of confidence that I had over myself.

Classes started and new set of subjects were introduced. Most subjects remained same apart from one or two which got spin off to new subjects. The teachers were busy teaching while I was busy checking whom I know and whom I don't in my class.

After few lessons, we had lunch break. I rushed to the corridor to check Shivyanka's class but she was nowhere to be seen. I saw Rakul and asked him if he had seen Shivyanka.

He said that she was in his class now and she had gone to school canteen as she forgot her lunch box. I cursed my luck; out of all the classes they had both, they were allotted the same class.

I thought the day couldn't get any worse but during cricket practice it was told that Rakul has joined the team as opening batsman, since the earlier one met with an accident. All the frustration of entire day affected my cricket practice where Rakul hit boundaries on all my balls. He did take a revenge of his wicket which I took during the cricket try outs.

I saw Shivyanka next day and asked how she was. But that interaction didn't last long since she was chosen for drama club and they had an event coming up.

I wanted to talk more but didn't get any chance throughout the day. But I didn't let my cricket practice get affected due to this. I had to maintain my position in the team since the tournament was now approaching and coach was replacing the non performing players.

Shivyanka and I talked in bits and pieces during the entire week but none we had that full-fledged talk where talked our hearts out.

Soon the team got letter from the principal that we had to skip classes for the practice sessions therefore for the remaining weeks of the month before the tournament we were told to be in school grounds throughout the day.

Leave alone talking to her, I didn't even get time to see her.

Practice sessions were hard, the sun used to shine brightly and we used to practice in the scorching heat.

All of us used to bath in sweat entire day. I used to be so tired when I reached home that I used to sleep without even taking the bath.

Mom used to wake me up in evening for snacks and then forcing me to bath. However, in mornings we had a privilege to arrive late in school since we did not have any classes to attend. Shyamak used to drop me to school and he used to buy fruits for me on the way which would help me to practice under the sun.

Each day of the session made the team stronger, efficient and effective. After the final day of the practice, we weren't just set of students who were chosen to play. We were a team which had a common heart and brain.

The first qualifier match of ten overs was in the city itself which we needed to win to enter into the tournament. I reached home after the final day of practice, packed my cricket kit, had dinner and slept early. The bus was supposed to pick me up at six in the morning.

I instructed Shyamak to wake me up at five in the morning and if I didn't wake up then to pour water on me. I woke up in Shyamak's first attempt and got ready for the match. I wore the school jersey. It felt like wearing the national cricket jersey.

It had my name written on back and a number '27'. Shyamak made juice, which I had to gulp down when I heard the bus honking at my security gate. Mom and dad were already awake and were waiting for me at the porch.

They wished my luck as I rushed to the bus and took my favorite back seat. The bus started and headed towards its destination. The school was located on the highway which was an hour drive from my place. I decided to sleep since I was really tired. The coach woke me up within few minutes informing that it would affect my performance and it was a match that we couldn't afford to lose.

It was really hard for me to control my sleep, I checked my handbag for some snacks and found few candies in it. I remember how dad used to have one driving late night, it helped them being awake. I took one and kept it in my mouth and it was then when I recalled even Shivyanka liked having them. She used to share it with me in the previous school but she never did in this one.

I didn't realize when I felt asleep while I was thinking all of this when the next thing I noticed was coach trying to wake me up. We had already arrived in school and team was getting down from the bus. I got down and saw the school.

The school was so small that three to four of these schools could fit in our school ground still leaving place for us to play football. We were directed towards washroom where we washed our faces and went to the ground for warm up. The opponent team was already there doing warm ups and all of them seemed to be seniors.

Soon, the match started and we won the toss. Aman who was the captain of our team chose to bowl first and I was sent to bowl the first over. The coach had high expectations from me. I took the ball and went to the crease. I did a run up and delivered the first off spin. The batsman defended his wicket, guess he was testing my potential because that was a pretty easy bowl. The next delivery returned with a ball passing by my face. It did touch my right ear though but I was lucky to be safe.

Umpire warned the batsman. The next of four balls went defense and the team scored two runs in the first over. I was sent back for fielding. I was given my next bowling in fourth over where the team had already scored twelve runs with zero loss of wickets. I got a wicket in that over but also gave six runs in that over.

The next bowling was given to me in seventh over where the team had scored forty-five runs with loss of two wickets. I gave a boundary in that over and few additional runs with zero wickets. The team's total was now fifty-five runs after my over. The coach didn't send me for the next over and the score after last over was seventy.

The opening from our team was done by Rakul and Aman. Both of them played really well and at least a boundary was hit in every over. They knew when to defend, and play loft shots or ground shots. The batsman met the target in eight overs and we headed to our way back to home after spending some gala time post match.

The next day Rakul and Aman were called upon the stage during the assembly for winning the qualifier round while the entire team standing amongst other children were ignored. It did pinch me but it also gave me motivation that I had to perform well to make up to the stage.

The next round of twenty over match was supposed to happen in our school. If we qualified this one, we were directly into the semi-finals. The team practiced harder since the opponents were defending champions and the coach didn't want us to lose.

We used to start practice early morning and used to reach home late. I used to get so tired that sometimes I even forgot to have my dinner.

The practice continued for a week when the match day was announced. It was supposed to be a day after so the team was given off for the day since all of us were exhausted.

The day arrived, the bus picked me up in the morning for school. I reached on time and the opponent team was already on the school grounds doing the warm up. Their bats and pads seemed to better than ours, no wonders they were defending champions.

Our coach always used to say that it's not the gears which make a player but it's his playing style. We needed to prove the same in the field today.

The match started with a toss which was won by the opponents who chose to bat first. I was told to field in the inner circle for the first few overs. The bowler for the first over threw fast deliveries but batsmen took few runs and a boundary in the first over. The score was nine in the first over itself which got increased in the second over to twenty-two for the loss of zero wickets. I managed to lower the run rate but giving four runs in that over. The fifth over witnessed a wicket, where Rakul took the catch for the ball thrown by me. By the time tenth over got over, the score was one hundred ten for one wicket. The next ten overs didn't give us any wicket and score was two hundred for the loss of one wicket.

The team tried best but maybe it wasn't our day we thought. The opening was done by Aman and Rakul. They were under immense pressure since then the entire school had collected on the ground to watch the cricket match. I noticed Shivyanka too cheering for the team.

Aman got out in the first ball since he tried to hit the boundary with bad timing. Seeing captain getting out was extremely demoralizing. Aman came back to the bench and other batsman was sent to assist Rakul. Rakul tried to get the strike in the first over and finished the over with a six. The score in first over was eight for one wicket. By the time we reached fifth over, the score was 48 for the loss of two wickets however, Rakul was still playing on the field.

The tenth over witness ninety-six runs for the loss of two wickets. Rakul completed his century in the twelfth over and the score was one hundred twenty by then. Rakul finished the match when four runs were need in one ball and he hit a six on a bouncer.

The team knew it was a fluke but no one said anything because we were in the semi-finals then. The teams were taken to dining hall where we were served with snacks and had photo sessions with fellow team mates. On reaching back to the field I saw Shivyanka approaching me. I thought she came to congratulate me but my smile vanished when she asked for Rakul. She wanted to congratulate her for wonderful innings. She went to him and gave him a handmade card with a chocolate.

That time it didn't feel like knife slitting my heart, it felt like a knife being pushed into my heart. I felt jealous. I wanted to be with her instead of that guy. For once, I forgot the fact that he was my cousin and planned to hit him with the ball I had in my hand but then I saw Shivyanka's smiling face and I didn't want to wipe it off.

I was so heartbroken after that match that I didn't play the semi-finals and finals. I told my dad to write an application to the school that I wasn't able to focus on my studies hence I need a break from the cricket tournaments.

By doing this, I made a genuine excuse to cut myself from Rakul and saving my blood relation with him.

I rarely met with Shivyanka in that academic year due to obvious reasons. Also due to regular cricket practice for the first tournament, I used to fall sick very frequently making it difficult for me to top the class that year.

I stood second that year and Shivyanka topped that year. Though I was sad with my bad marks but it was pea sized in comparison to the happiness I had for Shivyanka for bagging the first position.

Also, little did I know that I was seeing Rakul for one last time. Else I would have taken my kind of revenge way back then.

*****

'What happened to Rakul' I asked while having last biscuit on the plate.

'His parents moved to some different city' He replied.

'So you never met him again?' I added.

'In literal sense I didn't see him but I won't say that he didn't troubled my life again' said Siddhant.

It was three in the morning now and Siddhant went to washroom. I kept the dishes in the sink and checked my phone.

It had eight missed calls from Avni and number of unread messages. I forgot that I had kept my phone on silent mode. I tried calling her but her phone was not reachable. She must have slept I thought.

I read one of her messages and it read:

I miss us being together Devang. I know you have responsibilities on your shoulder but I don't want to be part of that burden. I want to share that burden with you forever. I want to wait for you at doorstep when you return from home. I want to cook for you when you arrive from office and sometimes even have a coffee with you while watching our favorite show. I want to live every moment of my life with you.

Avni used to send me these kind of messages every now and then. She was worried that I might stop giving time to her and would eventually break up with her. I didn't want that and in fact I loved her very much. But I wanted to excel further since my career had just started a few years back. I wanted to maintain the position where I was in the corporate world and I just couldn't afford any distractions.

Siddhant came back to the balcony and re arranged his bean bags. He lit his cigarette and took a small puff. He coughed a bit and placed the cigarette in the ash tray.

He wiped his glasses and started to recite the next part.

*****

CHAPTER 8

The School Trip

The new academic session for class eighth began and classes got re-shuffled again. It seemed like a chance of luck when me and Shivyanka were in the same class again.

The things slowly changed after Rakul moving out of the scene. Our talks initially used comprise generally of comparisons between me and him which seemed to be her favorite hobby. Every time, she would keep Rakul on the higher side which used to make me angry. She loved making me angry back then.

After the summer breaks, a week long school trip was organized to Dharamshala in Himachal Pradesh. Dharamshala is known was for its cedar forests on the edge of the Himalayas. This city is home to his holiness Dalai Lama. Various Buddhist monasteries and libraries are situated in the holy city of Buddhists.

I so wanted to go there but I had to seek permission from my parents. I didn't go on trips before and wanted to experience it. Later that night I asked my dad for permission and out of the blue he didn't allow.

I was like Fuck. He never said no for anything but why now. But instead of doing root cause analysis and stressing on it again and again, I decided to respect his decision and came back to my room sobbing in my bed.

It was then when Shyamak came to my room and explained the reason behind dad's decision. He said that he heard mom and dad talking about some urgent fund requirement which would lead to hampering the family budget for that month.

Shyamak over the period of time had proved to be more of a friend rather than the care taker. Sometimes I wonder what would have I done without his dose of advices.

I went next day with head hung low giving answer to my parent's decision on trip. Shivyanka's parents allowed her though. She said that she could convince my parents if I wished. But respecting my dad's decision was of utmost importance to me.

Everyone had that jolly mood on their faces while I was wishing all the time for my dad's decision to change. While fellow students were planning which all places they would visit and their sleeping plans in rooms, I was busy chalking down for classes which I had to take with left over children back in school.

The day arrived when all the children had to depart for the trip. When I carried school bag and wore school uniform, majority of the children carried their suitcase and wore casuals. Some of the students even spread rumors that my parents couldn't afford this trip and therefore they didn't allow me.

The only thing I could do was to ignore them. I didn't want to get into fight since it leads to nothing. The children departed through school bus during lunch time and I was left with handful children in class who were new joinees for that academic year.

I had no prior talks to them whatsoever, so I took this as an opportunity to make new friends. All of us used to share our lunch with each other. All of them liked the pasta that my mom made for me in school. I planned them to invite for lunch too but it went in vain since due to transportation issues. All in all, the time spent with them wasn't great but it was worth giving a shot, it felt like starting with a clean slate.

The school group returned from Dharamshala trip after a week during lunch time. They seemed to be tired but still had the glow of a wonderful trip on their faces. They had things to discuss while I struggled to connect with them and be on the same page.

Shivyanka was happy and was bubbling like a butterfly. She seemed to be on the zenith in the skies of happiness. I never saw her this happy before. What bugged me was her blush when she saw me in the classroom after returning from the trip and ran away.

Also, few of my classmates were looking at me in a suspicious manner as if I did something wrong behind their backs in school. I didn't know what was happening around me. Neither her blush would stop nor the eyes of suspicion looked away.

I managed to compromise in this changed environment for a week, but it bottlenecked in the next. I approached Shivyanka but she ignored with an awkward smile and ran away giggling, it got weirder.

I then approached her best friend Reshma Khan. Reshma was a short heighted fair complexioned girl who the most talked about girl in the entire eighth grade. She had looks that could make man do anything she wanted. But she never attracted me, don't know why.

So she was standing in the corridor filling her water bottle. Her hair was tied up in a bun and sleeves folded till elbow. I asked what the reason was for this awkward behavior of few children towards me. She laughed and confirmed if I was being innocent or I seriously didn't have any idea.

She then took me to one of the vacant classroom and sat one of the teacher's table. It looked awkward. If anybody would have seen us, we would have been in big trouble.

 She started narrating what all happened on the trip. She literally started to talk about each and every moment of the trip. I had to interrupt her and asked to cut to the chase. She then told the actual reason of Shivyanka's changed behavior towards me.

She told about a game which they on the last night of the trip. It was called Truth and Dare where a pen was spun and the one to whom the cap of the pen pointed had to choose between truth and dare. If truth was chosen, the person would have to tell truth about any question the other would ask. If other was chosen, a task was to be performed by that person.

When it was Shivyanka's turn, she chose truth. Reshma asked who was her crush in school. Shivyanka initially hesitated to answer the question but after insisting her again and again she took my name.

I was surprised by the answer. She never told or shared anything with me related to this and I didn't have any idea about this. After hearing this, I too started to blush and couldn't stare into Reshma's eyes anymore. Reshma further added that it was completely normal and these kind of feelings generally develop for each other due to attraction.

I could feel butterflies in my stomach as if I had waited to hear this since birth. The was jumping and hopping from inside whereas I had to act calm from outside. All the memories of our childhood flashed in front of my eyes and it all looked like as if the destiny had want us to meet and end up being together. My family's relocation, Rakul changing the school, it all looked connected.

I was so into the feel then that I didn't realize when Reshma left the room next I remember being poked by classmate with a compass. He was looking for me since half an hour and he found me staring at the window in some random class. He thought I had gone bonkers but little did he know what was going in my mind.

I went back to the classroom and found an angry teacher waiting for me. I knew I was in hot soup and I couldn't reveal the fact as to what I was doing all this time. I end up being punished by her but all seemed to be nothing when I saw Shivyanka blushing looking at me while I was facing the class with my hands up in the air.

After the class, we had recess where I went to her desk and signaled Reshma to leave us alone. I sat beside her and broke the ice revealing the fact was happened that day. The pink blush turned to red and she ran away to washroom.

I waited for her in the corridor when she returned back and requested her to accompany me to the canteen. I didn't want to have food or anything, I wanted to have private time with her. She didn't stop blushing which made her look cute. I didn't have any feelings for her before, I guess it was her helpful nature which made me fall in love for her, she saw the actual guy in me which others couldn't.

We entered the canteen and she asked what I wanted to have. I replied shyly that I wanted to have her. She gripped my arm and hugged it tightly. Never had anyone done like this before to me.

I took her to a corner table, corner enough to make us hard to notice. I held her hand and confessed my feelings for her. I told her that she was the one I wanted to be with like forever and also confessed the time when she drew the card for Rakul which made me burn like a hot volcano waiting to get erupted. I told her that I wanted to smash his head with the ball I had but that would have wiped the cute smile off her face. To which she kisses my hand went 'Awwwww'.

I don't understand what is the deal between girls and this word. Every time they see or hear something, they go 'Awwwwwww.

*****

It was four in the morning, the cups were empty, the ash tray was full of smoked cigarettes and my phone was almost out of battery.

I didn't know a man who looks perfectly fine from outside had so much to say and share. So he wasn't a stubborn boy since childhood. He was quite jolly full kind of child like most of us are. The only thing which was in my mind was if everything was so perfect what happened all of a sudden which changed everything in their life?

What was it which changed this man's life.

'So what happened next, did you guys end up being together for years?' I asked.

'Times Devang, you just can't change time and destiny. You think you have things under your control but actually its destiny which is playing its own game. You have to live in each and every moment of the life given to you. The sooner you understand the better it will be for you.' Siddhant said.

His words of wisdom both in company and in personal life put me in tough times. Tough times not because I couldn't understand what he said but because I didn't know how to implement it in real life.

'Letting your love go and not fight for it is the worst thing to do. People say to fight for your right. But what they don't say is fight for your love. If you actually love someone, it's your responsibility to be together and handle your part in a relationship properly' He added.

I did know what was about to come from the way his facial expressions changed.

*****

CHAPTER 9

The First Date

It had been almost two months of our relationship and we had grown immensely fond of each other. Shivyanka and I used to frequently hangout at her place.

She used to have a latest video gaming console which her dad got during this defense trip abroad. She was extremely fond of gamin. In fact, even me in my best form couldn't score more than her when she was in her worst.

It wasn't the fact that I was a bad player or something but she was really good player. She was in fact one of the top 100 national players of FIFA. She was never interested in those girly things after growing up. She never used any cosmetic apart from the essential ones. She was a natural beauty in herself which would get spoilt if any external makeup was applied to it.

We had similar taste of music. She used to come to my place for hearing K-POP, a Korean pop music genre. We didn't understand a single word of it, but what made us love it were the tunes. We also watched cartoon movies like Cars or Tom and Jerry. She was my Tom and I was her Jerry.

It may have looked cheesy but it was definitely better than the Babu and Shona used by other pairs of our age back then. Sometimes there were times when we didn't talk or not even exchange text for a day. But we were fine with it as long as we knew that other was there in the time of need.

We weren't just a couple; we were that mass which filled that empty space in each other's life.

Our love and fondness towards each other couldn't be kept hidden amongst students for a period of time. In fact, after the first month of our relationship students started talking about us. How we looked cute together and it was the perfect pair of two toppers. I would revert by saying that it I wasn't the topper and would never have been if that girl didn't make me realize my inner potential.

Though our parents loved each other but we still decided not to tell them as at the end of the day, we were kids studying in school. Also if not that, her parents were way too possessive about her.

I remember the first day we went on date and each and every moment lies fresh in my heart. Toughest part was to decide where to go. She wanted to go to ice cream parlor while I begged to differ from her opinion. Books was what fascinated me more than frozen milk in cups and cones. To decide this, we played a match of pen fight since we both were good at it. Whoever won would have the final call on the venue of the date.

The score was 5-4 for a five pointer match and I won with a border line margin. However, I didn't want our first date to be based on compromise so I decided to choose the third option which would be better for both of us, a movie date. A new animated movie released back then named 'Despicable Me', a story about a scientist and his funny set of assistants cum servants which were called minions.

The way we planned for it was also way weird and awkward. We had our mid-terms of class 8th and my parents had a strict no phone policy implied during exams. However, I had someone who would helped me to meet her, he was none other than Shyamak. He was gifted with a smartphone by dad on his birthday and I knew how it manipulate Shayamak to use it for my own benefit.

The only person my mom trusted amongst my friends was by bestie Ruhaan. He was a medium heighted innocent guy who was always into studies. He always helped me wherever and whenever he could. He didn't pass through society's expectation of hotness or smartness but his innocence would have won anyone's heart. His sincere attitude towards life is what made us best friends within months of him joining the school.

I called Shyamak a day before in my room and taught him how to use his phone's mail box. I set up a fake mail account by Ruhaan's name and sent a mail to myself which read:

'Hi Sid,

The exams are killing me. Let's go out for a movie. How about Despicable me at 8pm.

Meet me at walkway mall.

Regards,
Ruhaan'

Shyamak was way too innocent to understand this. I approached my mom to show her the mail that was sent by so called Ruhaan. By seeing Ruhaan's name mom didn't smell a fish and allowed me to go. Well this is what happens when your parents trust your best friends more than they trust you.

However, it was way too easy for Shivyanka. She just asked her parents that she was going out with Reshma and they allowed. There was no exchange of mails or anything between her and any fake accounts.

Well I could have used that too, but what was the fun without some struggle.LOL!

I was allowed to take my phone that day, so there were no issues in coordinating where and when to meet.

I tried dressing up in my best. I wore a blue open neck t-shirt and blue shorts with leaves print on it. Added were the floaters which gave a beachy look. Walkway mall was recently inaugurated in the city. Being the first mall in the city, it almost had all the facilities of a top notch mall of a tier-1 city ranging from a departmental store to a luxurious multiplex cinema.

I valued time back then too and reached exactly at 8pm when we were supposed to meet. However, I couldn't find her where I asked her to so I rushed at the box office to buy tickets.

I had a little pocket money at that time and was saving it to buy a video game. But no video game was worth the time I was about to have it with her. I paid all the money to the ticket teller that I had and got two tickets for the movie show.

I rushed back to the entrance of the mall where we were supposed to meet. There was a huge crowd at the security check waiting to come in and I couldn't find her in the crowd. Her number was switched off too.

I ran into the crowd to find her, just in case if she was in there. I got no success even after getting stomped on my toes and having an elbow on my face by a man who was in way too hurry to get in as if he had wanted to pee and couldn't find a washroom for that matter.

Just when I decided to leave and came out of the gate, I saw her standing near the parking lot. She looked really pretty. Her hair was open, she had applied lip gloss and a mascara. She wore a black sleeveless dress which looked perfect for the occasion. She noticed the way I was staring at her, ran towards me and gave me a tight hug. Well, it was the first time when she hugged me. It felt different, actually it felt lovely.

The way she smelt like roses which must be because of her perfume and her hair smelt fruity which was just mesmerizing. Her presence that day must have lit millions of lamps in my heart. Her silent big eyes told millions of phrases for love for me.

Yes, she was mine and I just couldn't have thanked God enough that day. It all seemed majestic and magical.

Little later I realized that we were getting late for the movie, I held her hand and took her in. A hand held so tight which wouldn't let her go even if millions of waves tried to wash us apart.

All the people stared at us in an awkward manner but it didn't matter to us since we were so into each other at that very moment. Little did I remember what was in the movie, because who would watch it when you have the prettiest girl in the world sitting beside you.

I saw her giggling, laughing and sometimes even staring back at me. All the hardships which I went through for this date seemed to be worth it.

It was ten already when we came out of the mall and went straight to the park which was just opposite to the mall. We sat on the bench and watched the twinkling stars saying their own story. The moon's light seemed to be nothing in front of her glow. A glow which would be enough to light thousands of dark villages of the country.

She looked at the stars while I looked at her.

This was the first time when she asked what did I want to be when I grow up. I had witnessed a transition from middle class to higher class during childhood and definitely the latter was far better than the first one.

I replied that definitely something which would give me lot of money in future. Her plans were completely different. She wanted to help the poor and give something back to the society.

She then promised that we would follow our dreams no matter what, even if we be together or not.

I dint know if it was the mood, the way she looked or these words which made me love her even more.

After few minutes, my phone rang up. It was my dad and wanted to know my whereabouts. She brought her car and her driver though. She dropped me home and then returned to her home.

I had asked her to text me up when she reached. My phone buzzed after half an hour. It had message from her:

- *Shivyanka: Thanks for the lovely day, Tom. You looked cute.*

- *Siddhant: Your welcome Jerry. You looked pretty too.*

- *Shivyanka: love you, don't ever leave me*

- *Siddhant: Love you too. I promise to be with you in your ups and downs.*

This was just our first date. After this we had number of dates during the year. From book shops to amusement park, we went everywhere.

Whenever we had bad mood, we found solace in other's company.

We didn't let relationship interfere with our studies. We both made it to the first position in the class that year and in heart of each other.

*****

I went aww after hearing all of this. Siddhant returned me with his annoyed look. He hated this when anyone did this in front of him.

'So what exactly happened next? I thought you guys were about to break up' I asked.

Siddhant's expression an hour back clearly reflected it. Had I made a mistake understanding him for the first time?

'Don't rush to things Devang, I was making up the mood before the turning point in the story' Devang said.

I witnessed the sun rising for the first time. My watch stroke 5:30 and the sky turned orange from light blue. We had been awake for entire night hearing tycoon's story.

'Let's go for a drive' Siddhant said. I asked him to wait, since driver wasn't available. He expressed his desire to drive rather than sitting on the back seat.

He changed his clothes while I washed my face. We locked his house and went down to the basement parking. He pressed the unlock button and the beast beeped. I used to call his car beast, because it resembled closely to a black bull.

We sat in and he turned the engine on. Slowly he took the car outside the basement and then gave a full acceleration to it. In a minute, a car was turned into a rocket driving past the lanes. He loved driving, especially when he had someone to talk to.

Business had kept him away from this hobby of him and he wanted to compensate for all the lost time.

I requested him to slow down the car and to continue the remaining part. He ignored my words and drove straight to the highway. After driving madly for the another one hour, he stopped outside a tea stall and ordered two teas.

He then took the water bottle out of his car to rinse while I arranged for a place to sit. He grabbed the tea cups and kept on his car.

He ordered me to stop making seating arrangement and told me to sit on the hood of the beast.

He took a sip from his cup and started to narrate again.

*****

CHAPTER 10

Lines, Vines And Crying Times

The relationship went smoothly for a year almost. We were a cute happy couple which had world of our own having own goals and freedom. No one was supposed to get into it and destroy it for us.

Little did we know that this happiness was only left for some point of time. It all would end soon for us.

One day after returning from our dinner date, I decided to text her. It was really late that night. I guess it was already two or three in the morning then.

- *Siddhant: Hey! Sleeping?*

The message went unanswered. After almost an hour my phone buzzed.

- *Shivyanka: What is it Reshma? Why are you disturbing me at this point of time?*

- *Siddhant: It's me Siddhant. Why are you calling me Reshma?*

- *Shivyanka: Oops, it must be appearing due to some technical snag.*

- *Siddhant: Thanks for the date today, it was lovely. Love you! sweetie pie. Good night ...XOXOXO*

I didn't get a reply from her end after this message.

Next day during a class, I asked her as to why didn't she reply to my last message. What followed next totally surprised me and seemed as if the world had gone topsy turvy for me.

She said that she didn't get any of my messages that night. In fact, she forgot her phone on the dining table after reaching home. She didn't see it in the morning either. I told her about the entire scenario as to how I received her reply on my cellphone during the night when I was texting her and she mistook me to be Reshma.

She further added that she had saved my number on her phone as Reshma. It helped her to come on dates with me as she used to show the invitation messages to her mom by her name. Her mom used to allow by reading the name itself.

I couldn't understand what was happening. I did get messages on my phone that night from her number and I did reply too on the same number after that.

I was so worried that I bunked the next class and took her too with me and sat in the canteen. I explained her entire situation and gave step by step account about the entire incident that happened.

She did some thinking around it and her expressions seemed to change within few minutes. She told that she didn't see the phone not because she was getting late or she didn't want to but the phone was not on the table. Also, her mom had the habit of waking up at four in the morning for Yoga and other exercises.

In fact, when she was leaving home today, her parents were talking in a closed room and didn't even say bye to her while she was leaving for school.

I also realized that it was around four in the morning when I received her text.

Thinking and talking further on this, it was deduced that her mom must have seen my messages on her phone and replied on it thinking it was Reshma. Things turned worse, when I texted my last message to her.

She began to cry and I got scared too. We didn't know what to do and how to react. We could have informed about this relationship to our parents long back, had we been mature enough. When the things were going perfectly fine, we ended up spoiling them up.

For the rest of the day we sat in canteen planning to tackle this situation. Even spending full day things of various permutation and combinations, we got to nothing. We realized that we had to face it and had no other options.

She lost her cool and started to talk rubbish like jumping from roof or getting drowned into the school pool. That was not even the last thing I wanted her to do. In fact, I loved her so much that I was ready to hear a hard one from my parents too.

I had to be strong in order to support her. I decided to drop her home first and then going to mine. We didn't take school bus that day. We took an auto to her place. Her eyes were sore and she couldn't stop crying. She had already made my shoulder wet but it was something which I was least concerned to.

During the entire journey she kept asking me one question, was it that we were seeing each other for the last time. I didn't know how to answer that. There was quite a chance that it was all a bad assumption and maybe someone else used her phone to reply. But no one apart from her parents lived in that house.

Also, we were too big to believe in ghost and shit. The auto driver gave me a suspicious look which could be seen from the rear view mirror. I ordered him to look straight and follow the direction to the destination. What was happening in our life was not something to be entertained off.

I didn't want this journey to end, because it might had been the last journey we were having together. But it wasn't a dream world now, we were in the real world and this journey did end. We reached outside her house.

I paid the driver with money I had in my pocket. I was saving this for our movie tonight but who knew that it won't happen. I asked her to go in and kissed her forehead. On reaching the gate, she looked back at me again with a hope for us meeting again soon. I couldn't stop myself and ended up crying on the road itself.

She ran towards me and hugged me. Gave me her handkerchief and asked me to wipe tears with it. I asked what if it was our last meeting that day.

She said that even if we don't meet, we would leave it all on the destiny. If we are meant to be, then we will be together again.

In the meanwhile, if we don't end up being together after that day, we promised each other that we would follow our dreams that we talked about in the park during our first date.

She hugged me for the last time that day and went back in. She didn't turn back after that. With our lovely memories of last one year flashing in front of my eyes, I headed on my way to home. I had someone waiting there too.

On reaching home, I found my mom smothering in anger. Well Indian mothers can be sweet, but when they are angry one should better not fool around with them. She was sitting on the sofa waiting for me as I walked in.

She got up, came up to me and slapped me really hard. The slap was so hard that I could hear static for almost a minute. Shyamak was not there in the home that day, he went to his village to help his father with something, else he would have tried protecting me. But I actually did deserve this slap on my face.

I lied to my parents for almost a year that I was out with Ruhaan when actually I was dating her all that time. She said I had disappointed her badly and their family's reputation is messed up because of me. Soon came my father and he scolded a hell lot of things to me too. Just because of me had to leave his office in the middle of day to deal with this situation.

They were not angry because I had a girlfriend. They were angry because I hid it from them. I didn't dare to ask who did they knew about the incident. It was clear enough that Shivyanka's mother must have called up my mom to tell about our relationship.

Dad also said that he had invested lot of efforts to see me grow and learn but it all seemed to go down in drain now. The scolding and beating stopped after a while and I ran to my room sobbing. I locked the door and started to cry loudly.

After few minutes, mom's phone rang up. It was Shivyanka's dad and he wanted to speak to me. Mom darted into my room and threw her phone on me. I picked up my phone and as I mummed a word her dad began shouting on me.

He abused me and my family that hurt me the most. His words were so foul and dirty that I didn't hear most of the words in my entire life. His anger was justified too. Her daughter cheated on her because of me.

It was me who was to be blamed and not her. Had I not taken the first step a year back, we would just have been friends and things would have been fine between us. But it was me who wanted to be in relationship with her and also wanted to lie to the parents.

Neither anyone in my family slept that night nor they had anything to eat during this entire scenario. I cried on the floor sitting in the corner of my room for the entire night. I wanted to speak with her for the one last time.

I wanted to hug her and tell her that I loved her most. My phone, laptop and every gadget I had was confiscated. My own house felt like a jail. I could hear mom dad talking in the other room that how I was a shame for their family and how my schooling should be dropped.

All the hard work which was done in all these years and all the laurels got for school went in vain due to one mistake that we made. I felt my life sinking from my hand like sand. The more I tried to hold it by tightening the grip, the more quickly it slipped away.

I didn't go to school next day due to obvious reasons. All the marks of beatings I got on the other day were still clearly visible on the body, teaching me a lesson as to what all can happen if you hide things from your parents.

The things didn't improve next day, rather they got worse. The morning started with the bad note when Dad approached my room and scolded me again. Next he said that he won't be talking to me for the rest of his life and if I wanted to, then I was allowed to leave his house forever. It can be said that he literally tried to disown me by saying this.

Mom on the other hand said that she doesn't want to see my face again. The only thing she would do was to make food for me and rest I would have to manage alone. I didn't have food the entire day and it was night soon. Due to my emotional distress I lost the track of time and didn't realize when it was morning again.

I had a quick bath, applied some ointment on the marks and rushed to my bus with the only uniform I had in almirah. The students' reaction after looking at me in the class was self-explanatory that they knew about the entire situation.

But I wonder who would have told it to them. I looked for Shivyanka but she hadn't reached the school by then. I went to Reshma and asked where she was. She ignored me completely. I then went to Ruhaan's desk and he explained me the entire thing.

On the day before, Shivyanka's father was looking for me in school. Later he came to class and told everyone that Shivyanka was now moving to Mumbai to her relative's place and would never return back.

I broke down after hearing this and started to cry. The condition worsened and I was sent to medical room since I had fainted for not having anything for 2 days.

I was hospitalized for a day in the hospital and my parents were called up in school for counseling sessions. They were told that I had learnt my mistake and I should be forgiven. It would hamper my performance and studies in these crucial years of life if not dealt properly.

Though things didn't change over a period of time, but they did improve. Dad didn't talk to me for a really long period while I found a space in mom's heart again. Over a period of time I learnt my lesson to not to hide things from my parents specially if they were as sensitive as a relationship.

However, in the series of next few months, I got to know that Shivyanka wasn't sent just because she lied to her parents. She was sent because her parents didn't like me. They thought that I was not capable to match their standards of living and I would be a disgrace to their family if Shivyanka ends up with me.

Therefore, in order to save their family name and status, she was sent to Mumbai to pursue her further studies.

CHAPTER 11

The Marriage

A year had passed since that incident and I had no news of her. Things were normal now, however I wasn't able to top that year. The fact that I managed to pass was nothing short of a miracle in itself.

I had been given various counseling sessions in school since then to avoid and train me for any kind of such happening in future.

What everyone failed to understand was this was true love and not a mere infatuation. Though I didn't tell anyone but I still prayed for her in every breath I took wishing for her to be okay. Every game I played reminded of her whenever I used to be one of the top scorers in my area.

People say that you move on with time but what if you have lost the track of time after your partner has went away. I wasn't able to focus on studies like I used to do.

The only thing which flashed in front of my eyes was her crying face which she had before entering into her house. Her promise that we would follow our dreams were the only words which used to pump in my ear drums every now and then.

I tried talking with few of my friends who moved to Mumbai but all of them said the same thing. Mumbai was too big for people to be found just by name.

But thanks to Mark Zuckerberg and his team that FB soon rolled out to the entire world. Within the day of its launch I made my account on it. In fact, I was the first one in my class to have FB account. Everywhere in the news it read that FB was a medium to connect with your friends.

So, I used it as an opportunity to connect with Shivyanka. I typed her name 'SHIVYANKA' in the search bar and got 1000+ results, it was impractical for me back then to go through each and every result. I tried adding her surname to it and typed 'SHIVYANKA JUNEJA' and still had 100+ results on my screen.

With the internet speeds we had back then, only 10-15 FB accounts could have been checked on a single day. I didn't mind that. I used to check each and every account with a hope to be her but most of the time I ended up sending request to wrong Shivyanka or a fake account which was operated by a different person altogether.

I used to do this exercise for every day until one day I got a request from an ID name 'TOM' and had a pic of K-POP band member on it. I definitely knew it was her. I kept her nickname 'Tom' and we loved K-POP.

I accepted her friend request and sent her a message over messenger. She saw and ignored it. I sent her again which went unanswered.

After a day she replied back asking how I was and what I had been up to for past 1 year. I told her that I was annoyed how she left me alone in misery and I had nothing to do with my life after that. She told that things took a different turn for us back then, a turn which none of us would had expected.

She said that she had flunked a year in school there since she was mentally disturbed after this incident and wasn't able to concentrate on her studies. Her parents were disappointed with her marks and had decided to keep her their permanently.

We talked for normally for few weeks where none of us confessed feelings for each other again. She once told that Rakul was in Mumbai too now and lived near to her place. They in fact are making plans to meet up soon.

Out of all the people in the world, he makes me angry and she took his name. I couldn't comment on him when she sent me a happy smiley after this message. Well if she was happy, I had no right to be sad. Because at the end of the day I wanted her happiness.

However, I didn't tell my mom that I was talking to her. After all the complications we had, it would might make the things worse again. Also, it was just normal talks this time and no one was commenting on any feelings of love whatsoever.

Another week had passed in the normal talks, when she broke me the news that she was returning back to the city for some family marriage. She wanted to know if we could meet anytime soon after that?

I had only one person to discuss this with, Ruhaan. Ruhaan over this period of one year had helped me to get my shit together and keeping my life back on track again. Shyamak had left the job as caretaker and joined his father in the village to provide help in his farms.

I called up Ruhaan that night and asked if he could help me to decide if meeting her was an appropriate option. On hearing this, Ruhaan got angry and his anger was clearly reflected in his voice. He told that there was no point in meeting her since whenever we have met or did anything together, we got stuck in complications and meeting up again would invite more in future.

I don't know how stupid I was to ignore his suggestion and agreed to meet her up. The only day that we could plan was the marriage day so we had to make sure we met right before the marriage. It was an afternoon affair so we decided to meet up in morning.

I didn't sleep a night before in excitement to meet her. An excitement which along with anxiety got lot of butterflies in my stomach. Every time I thought of her during that night made me blush. I didn't want to remember the time where we separated from each other. I wanted all the happy memories to remain.

The next morning, I took my cycle out and cycled to her house. This time we made sure that all of our conversations was done on messenger so that only we had access to it. I pinged her when I reached outside her home and waiting for her to sneak out from her home.

Over a period of time, her looks changed completely. She had grown out to be more fair, her hairs were longer and darker and she looked more of a lady now instead of a girl. Guess, puberty had a good effect on her.

She signaled me to meet her at next block to avoid any suspicion. I cycled to the next block and waited for her again. She hugged me from behind and her hands were on my chest.

I wanted to hold her hands and hug her back but I stopped myself and removed her hands. She asked what was wrong with me and if I was okay. I told that I just couldn't handle all of it again.

I couldn't keep my parents under the dark roof of lies this time. She laughed at me and asked me to chill. She told that we were kids back then and acted up in a foolish manner by being into a relationship.

Though I didn't want a relationship with her anymore now but this did hurt me one way or the other. I asked if she remembered the promise that we once made from each other if we wouldn't see each other again.

Her reply got me thinking that was it even a relationship back then. She told that she didn't remember any promise that we made from each other. I wanted to cry right there itself but I had to control it. It all felt like a big mistake but I couldn't say anything to her on this because she was smiling and was happy after a long period of time.

We talked about our lives since that incident and how the things have changed over a period of time for us. We talked for an hour until when we decided it was better we left for home now to avoid any suspicion.

With a heavy heart I bid her adieu with a promise of seeing her again in the future.

On reaching home, I checked my messenger which had a message from her. It read:

How can you think I can forget that promise that I once made from you? I know you must be working on your way to become rich. I am also looking forward to with some NGO after my graduation.

See you soon Jerry.

PS: You look hot now :-P

Soon after her relative's marriage we started to talk more frequently over messenger. She still loved games and was in fact better than what she had been earlier. She was participating in international gaming conclaves and wining trophies for the country.

We used to talk normally until after few months she asked if I still loved her. I confessed my feelings for her which made the situation weird initially but she later on reciprocated too by saying that she had always loved me and always wanted to have me in her life.

But still I didn't know if It was the relationship I wanted or just a casual friendship. I didn't want to ruin it that time. It felt like my last chance with her. A chance if spoilt again would make me lose her forever.

Therefore, I decided to take it slow. Also, Shivyanka only confessed her feelings for me. She didn't say that she wanted to be with me again.

We had to set few ground rules first to avoid any kind of complications this time. Some of them were that talks were to be strictly done on messenger and no communication with each other was to be done if anyone of us was in home.

We created fake account of each other to talk on messenger. Also, just to keep a double check, we archived our chats at the end of the day.

All in all, the plan was foolproof making it completely difficult for anyone to track that we were still in touch.

Ruhaan set a messenger group for all four of us Shivyanka, Reshma, Ruhaan and me. We used to have late night conversations with each other. Conversations regarding K-POP, movie or gaming. It was as if Shivyanka and me needed something to talk about and we would flood the chatroom with our messages.

Most of the time, it was only both of us who ended up chatting in the group. Reshma and Ruhaan just couldn't fit in. They thought that our conversations were pointless and meaningless. T

hose meaningless conversations were composed of thousands of unsaid words which only Shivyanka and I could understand.

*****

It was nine in the morning now and we were still on the highway by the tea stall. Siddhant's story made me drink 5 cups of tea and few stale biscuits too.

'Nice! Mr. Mastermind' I exclaimed. It was a happy life I believe.

'Alas! That happiness didn't last long' Siddhant said in sorrow.

'What happened? You guys were doing perfectly fine, weren't you' I questioned.

'Well Devang, life tends to play with you and you tend to make fool out for yourself if you get stuck in that game.' I didn't understand a word he said but it seemed in relation to the next part of the story he was about to recite

*****

CHAPTER 12

The Final Separation

All four of us were like a small happy family where Reshma and Ruhaan were like the pillars who supported this family. Had they not supported us, it would have been tough again to continue with Shivyanka.

We felt complete with each other and understood other's point of view. Reshma, Ruhaan and me completed school at the same time and through the same class whereas Shivyanka who flunked an entire year had to meet us up again.

All three of us moved to Delhi after passing out for school for higher education while Shivyanka remained in Mumbai to complete her twelfth.

We hung out together and sent pictures to Shivyanka. She in turn would get jealous and scolded us to stop hanging around until she completed her twelfth. But as expected, we didn't listen to her.

However, after moving out and living alone in Delhi changed few things like I didn't archived any of our chats and she could text me whenever she could. I wasn't even concerned about my cellphone being unlocked because I had my complete long deserved privacy now.

Mom usually used to ask every now and then that if was I still in touch with her. I used to lie her by saying that I don't have a clue of her and had no idea what was happening in her life.

The period of one year passed on its own pace and all the wait seemed worth it when I got the news from Reshma that Shivyanka has passed her twelfth with flying colors. In fact, she stood second in her state. Later that day, she posted on our messenger group that she was now coming to Delhi and was planning to leave Mumbai on which her parents had already given a prior permission.

Exile of three years seemed to end when she arrived at the airport and the trio was already there to receive her. What followed next was Rakul coming from next flight. He was granted a Letter of Recommendation from his college in Mumbai for a top business university in. Therefore, without even talking properly with her, I had asked them to leave and asked Reshma to text me Shivyanka's address once she got a place to live. Delhi.

Mom had already convinced him to live with me to keep a check on what I did in Delhi. Whenever, Rakul and I crossed paths in the cycle of life, my life had been on a roller coaster ride.

Rakul had no idea that I was in talks with her and I had to take him in confidence before I could reveal the fact to him. Else, he would directly report it to my parents.

I picked his bags and took him to my room in the city. It was a one-bedroom apartment located near Noida. It was near to my college which saved me travel time which was then invested in studies.

I asked him to get fresh while I made tea for us. I asked him to join me in the dining room where two hot cups of tea were waiting to be sipped. He sat on one of the chairs of the dining table and switched on the TV. He started changing channels frequently making it difficult for me to concentrate. I snatched the remote from him and he gave me an angry look. I tried to control the situation by telling that I was having a headache and wasn't in a mood to watch anything. I further asked how his family was and how had his life been in Mumbai.

I seriously had no intentions to ask any of it since I hardly cared what was happening in his life. Had he been not my cousin I would have kicked his ass and threw him out of the house since he was the one to whom Shivyanka was attracted once.

I waited for the perfect time to reveal the secret but couldn't find any that day since he was so tired that he slept for the rest of the day after our tea talks.

The next day, my phone buzzed early morning and found that Rakul was looking at the notifications. I got up immediately and snatched my phone from his hand. That cunt, didn't respect anyone's privacy since childhood.

I shouted at him saying that she shouldn't check anyone's phone without permission. He looked at me with sparkling eyes making it enough to understand the fact that my secret was now out in open.

He asked me if I still loved her the way I used to do it. I thought it was a loop hole and he was playing his own set of tricks. If I had said yes, he would have definitely taken it to my parents. Thus I replied in negation and still requested him to keep it a secret between us.

He was so happy after hearing this as if he had been released from jail. I asked why was he jumping and hopping around. He said that even he loved her and didn't confess his feeling because of me.

Out of all the girls in this world, how did he managed to find her as his love. Why couldn't he just have had crush on anyone else. Though I know that Shivyanka was prettiest, but why her. I couldn't take back the words I said to him earlier that I loved her. It would make it awkward.

To avoid hearing her name from in his voice again and again, I strictly instructed him not to talk about her whenever I was with him to avoid any awkward situations.

I didn't speak a word regarding this to Shivyanka. Rakul had made me swear that she shouldn't know that he had feelings for her. Since he wasn't sure about the feelings that he had for her.

The life was going well, another person was added to our family of four, Rakul the one to make it a jive of five. All four of us used to made sure that we don't reveal anything in front of Rakul, which could get us all in trouble.

Gradually time passed and I got internship in one of the leading companies of my management division. This internship would help me out to my way forward in corporate life and would give me various learning opportunities. The other four managed to get internships too and started to plan things accordingly.

Rakul's internship made him head back to his home for some time again leaving four of us back again the way we were. Ruhaan got internship in the city itself, Reshma and Shivyanka got internship back in the hometown and mine happened to be in Bangalore.

It was a tech company which provided back end support to e-commerce websites for their successful operations. My work was to assist the core operations team in drafting cost effective solutions for these companies.

I still had a week after arranging for my accommodation in the city. So I decided to head back to my hometown and enjoy that one happy last week with family before I fly to the concrete jungle in the tech city of India.

My day in hometown used to be pretty simple which would start quite late when my mom used to wake me up for bed tea. Post which I would go out for a walk and come back for lunch. After which I watched few shows on the television before my evening nap which would get interrupted when hunger stroke.

The habit of still living in full privacy turned out to be dangerous for me. One day while I was sleeping during the evening with my phone unlocked my phone buzzed. I knew it was her and before I could grab it, my dad got the hold of it. Look at the fate, I forgot to archive the chats for entire day and dad read each and every word of it.

Before I could do or say anything, I already had a red mark of his hand on my face. I tried my best to convince him the fact that I wasn't in relationship with her but he just wouldn't listen. The only option I had was to connect him to Rakul. He told that I was only talking to her casually like a friend and I had no intentions of getting her back in my life.

Each and every word pinched deep in my chest. Though this is what I told to Rakul once, but this completely was nothing what I felt. I loved her more than my life and would always do. No other girl would prove to be better than she was for me.

My dad then called his family and informed them about the entire incident. I felt helpless again. I couldn't do anything. I could imagine her crying and shedding tears. I felt that I had given her lot of pains and it was for the benefit of both that I leave her forever. She would definitely find someone better who would take care of her and didn't make her cry the way I did. I over thought it so much that I realized the call got over when dad came up to me and said that I would never talk to her or her family whatsoever.

Also I was told that after my internship I would settle permanently in Delhi and would return back to town only when necessary.

By the end of that day, Reshma came to my house with a sad news that Shivyanka is now been sent to Singapore for her education. Her dad has used his references to arrange a college for her there. Also, all her numbers and social networking accounts are deleted.

I learnt that I had lost her forever. Even if I tried, I couldn't get back to her and take her with me forever. The journey which started off as a childhood friendship and went up to a relationship where we had our share of joys and sadness was about to end and I couldn't do anything to stop it.

Leaving for Bangalore the next day, I called up Rakul. I knew the only one who would help me in this tough time was him, since he felt the same of Shivyanka what I felt. I asked him to promise me that he would take care of her and would compensate for all the sadness she had gone through and tears she had to shed being with me.

What that bitchy boy said next forced me to look him in a positive manner. He said that he won't be able to compensate for all the smiles she had being with me; he wouldn't be able to return back the comfort to her which she had whenever we used to call each other; he won't fit in my gaming shoes, because she wouldn't lose intentionally just to see him winning.

I couldn't believe my ears when I heard him saying this. The guy whom I hated the most said best things about my relationship. I never looked at the positive side that he had. We could have been good friends had I not screwed up this time.

After thinking for a while about what all he said, I switched off my phone for the one last time in my little Haldwani. I didn't know when would I see that city again in my life.

With the deep heart, I sat inside the plane which ran through the run way and flied high in the sky. I saw the city where I had spent most years of my childhood getting smaller and finally vanishing in front my eyes as the plane hid itself in the clouds.

The heart was full and I wished to cry. But I kept myself strong with a hope that my new friend Rakul was there for her whenever she cried.

*****

It was ten almost. I had spent my last 12 hours with this man hearing his personal stories and not a minute I faced when I got bore or found anything to be fake.

The thing which I observed during this entire narration was, that people always complaint about relationships cursing them to be complicated and heartbreaking. However, the pair tries to keep it simple since all they need is love and support from each other.

What makes it complicated are the people dealing outside the relationship. Had their parents understood the love and affection for each other, it would have been a way simpler that what it had turned out to be. A simple story where two people made for each other end up being together and live a happy life thereafter. But who can fight destiny and the plans it has made for us.

I won't also say that Siddhant didn't try to fight for her girl. He was too young then to think at this level but he was definitely mature enough to support her and being with her during that tough time.

After all these years and hearing this story of his, I can say that Siddhant still misses her even though he doesn't show it on his face. Deep somewhere down, he is still that little back bencher who is waiting for her fairy like Shivyanka to be back in her life again.

However, his story made me realize that if you encounter a true love, then never let it go. Just hold on to it even if it's hard, because what comes with the true love is hope. A hope of never to part.

Just then, I realized it was never a best time to do this.

I took my cellphone out, connected it to car charger and texted Avni:

'Sorry for not realizing how important were you in my life. I love you to moon and back. Let's plan to meet soon and finalize the step forward to being together forever'

'Whom are you texting' asked Siddhant still lied down on the car seat.

'Doing something what I should have done long time back' I replied with a blush.

'So what happened next?' I asked.

'It has been ten years since then. I moved to Bangalore for internship and further I joined Chanakya School of Management for higher management studies. Ruhaan and Reshma went out of touch after the split, I tried looking for them in various parts of the country but got no sign of them. I don't have any idea about Shivyanka. But once I had a word from Rakul that she has started some NGO. They were in serious relationship too but broke up after engagement' Siddhant said.

'She had spoilt the name of my family by breaking up with her and I hate her for that' He added.

HATE!! Did I hear that correct? So does this guy love her or hate her. Well, he she again managed to confuse me with his complex mindset.

*****

CHAPTER 13

Saving The Relation-Ship

Siddhant gave me an off that day for being a good listener to his so called tragic love story. I saw it as an opportunity to mend my sinking relationship with Avni. She was not some model looking hot shot kind of a girl. She was an innocent girl who belonged from a traditional Indian family who lived back in the village.

She had wheatish complexion, wore rimless specs on those big dark brown eyes. She looked perfect in Indian suits. She would have been first choice for any parents seeking a bride for their daughter. My mom and dad were no different, they would have loved to make her my wife had I told them about my relationship. Climbing corporate ladder and being a top business advisor has been my only priority till now, making it difficult for me to devote my time in this relationship I had with her.

Avni worked in Siddhant's company as a senior manager in Risk Advisory Department which was under my portfolio. I met her during her interview sessions where she proved that no candidate would be more perfect for this job then her.

I didn't fell for anyone's physical appearence, it was the brains which attracted me and Avni had some nice brains. She completed her post-graduation from Indian Institute of Management with flying colors. The marks didn't catch my attention, what caught my attention was her way of approaching and answering practical problems which were asked during the interview.

She believed in correcting the things from root, making it easy to implement new strategies at top level.

Her hard work during the years in the company proved my decision to be right and double promotions made sure that she was compensated well for her work and contribution.

So it all started when she joined as an assistant manager. I had already fallen for her during the interview. I requested Siddhant to allow her to directly report to me. Well you are entitled for some advantages when your friend is the owner of a multi-million conglomerate. Siddhant understood the motive behind my extra concern towards her which ended up by giving her the approval.

She used to work in her best capabilities and adhered to stringent timelines even if it required working in odd hours. The stringent timelines and the pressures were the source of examination to verify if was she actually the one made for me.

I wanted to tell how I felt for and no other option seemed to be better than by proposing her in her own style. It was a peak season and team was undergoing through lot of pressures. I scheduled my meeting with her and prepared a fake presentation on some impractical targets which were ordered to achieve by Siddhant.

She wore a white suit and her hair were open that day. She used lenses instead of specs which added to her cuteness. So while I was briefing her up with the targets which were almost impractical to achieve in real life, she broke down and started to sweat. That was my trigger point.

I immediately jumped to the last slide which had a proposal message. It said:

'I know these targets are hard to achieve. In fact, these are not even targets, these are just some random numbers which look nice in this presentation.

Relax, I just wanted to tell you that I love you and if you are with me these numbers are nothing, we could achieve anything which is impossible.

My assistant manager, I would seek your honor to be the chairman of my life and take control of it now'

When she finished reading this, I had already kneeled down, waiting for her reply. She said that though she didn't see me in the shoes of her lover till now, but she wouldn't mind trying me out.

Hearing this, I hugged her tightly. It was first time when I was so close to someone that even the air would have struggled to pass between us. Without any further ado, I grabbed her hand and took her at a café which was located near office. Spending some private time in office can be dangerous especially when you are reporting directly to the owner. Over the period of time, my care and concern for her made her fall in love with me.

We sat on the table and started to talk on how I fell for her and rest is history.

Coming back to present, I booked a cab to her place immediately after leaving from Siddhant's place since I was too tired to drive.

During the cab ride, I thought to myself for what I had been working my ass off if the person I love, the one with whom I want to spend my eternal life doesn't want to be with me anymore, what was the meaning of all that money and corporate progress that I had earned if I was not able to spend all of it with my love, while thinking all about it I made up my mind to propose her but I was still in a dilemma, to what if she says no and gave the lame excuse that every girl gives to end a relationship, that I didn't spend time with her.

No, what was I thinking; we both love each other she won't say no I knew that for sure, she will understand the reason why I have been working rigorously all the time to earn all this money.

Soon I reached her place with all these questions in my mind rhyming in a symphony and making me more and more nervous to approach her door.

I knocked on her door and there she was in her night wear without any makeup looking as gorgeous as ever, seeing her all my worries vanished in an instant.

That was now or never situation I kneeled down but fuck I forgot to bring the ring. How was I going to propose now, sitting on my knees and all confused I still chose to propose her.

The moment I proposed her, she started crying, wait a second had I done something wrong, did I proposed her in a wrong way, was she angry or what, even before I could say anything she kneeled down and kissed me on the lips, her lips were so soft and tender.

Then I know how it felt to kiss, i understood why people said "I want to eat your lips" I could taste her cherry lipstick, and she stopped, wait I sought more I wanted to taste those juicy lips again I wanted to suck them, I was looking at her like a kid whose candy which had been taken away from him. But wait she kissed me, so that means she do want me and we can be together.

Without any further delay I got up and reached her lips kissed them and even sucked those juicy lips and in response she started kissing me harder, and even started using our tongue.

In between all this kissing she took me in her house grabbed my shirt and tore off its buttons, we were going wild, her nails scratched my back. I never knew the pain during sex would be something to be enjoyed for.

I pulled her up and let her sit on the table . She took of her shirt while her lips were still on to me, she moaned, her moaning made me more excited. I couldn't resist myself and my hands slipped down under her pants.

Her moaning became even more sexy in response she pushed me back and pulled my pants my down which made me fall on the floor. She was holding what I would call something hard in her hands and started to play with it.

After a wild sex, she collapsed over me, oh god! Even though she was exhausted she still looked gorgeous, looks to die for I should say.

I headed back home in a taxi I booked while leaving from her place. During the entire time in taxi, I was thinking how a girl affected this man's life. But in real, did she actually loved her the way he did. Was Siddhant her infatuation?

Siddhant lived up to the promise which day did with each other before separation by being one of the richest man in the country. But what about her, was she actually working in some NGO or doing some social welfare?

I reached home and slept throughout the day. During the last 24 hours, life has shown me its various phases. One, don't ever let your true love go; Second, always be honest while dealing with different persons which get affected due to relationship; Third; always carry condoms when you propose someone, you may make out after that…kidding.

After waking up later that night I called up mom and asked her to come to Delhi, and told her I had a surprise waiting for her. I don't know what is on with our moms as if they have some chipsets installed in their minds which immediately triggers what their child is about to say because when I told about the *'Surprise'* she immediately replied that she is okay with a girl as long as she doesn't drink or smoke.

Like seriously, how can someone relate a surprise with son's bride to be. Well mom's condition was irrelevant because she didn't even touch any of these. In fact, she made me stop using all of these too.

After calling my mom, I went through my mail box and it had around hundreds of unread mails, comprising from audit reports, management information dashboards, funding proposals of startups and other daily work mails. But one thing out of all the mails that caught my eye was a sponsorship requirement which was sent by an NGO by the name of *'Akash Kiran Society'*.

It was the first time when I saw an NGO sending a mail for the sponsorship to us. Even though we did various tasks under CSR but still we were treated as the capitalist company which dealt only in numbers. Therefore, no NGO ever approached us, due to a mindset that it will be rejected.

As I was about to open the mail, the doorbell buzzed and I logged out from the system. It was none other than Avni, she got dinner of me. She closed the door from behind, put the dinner bag in the kitchen and came directly to my room. She opened my almirah and arranged the clothes in it.

'What are you doing?' I asked.

'I am making a place for both of us. I love keeping things neat and clean. So you should learn to do this from now on. Also, stop ordering food from outside, I will get it every day for you' she said with a bubbly face.

I could see a confidence in her eyes and a trust which she now had on our relationship. My attempt to save the relationship didn't go in vain I believe. A relationship required equal contribution from both the people and my contribution was far behind to what she had been contributing. My seeds of little attempt to save it today, started bearing fruits of success by night.

She arranged my almirah and then microwaved the food that she got for me. She served it on plates and placed it on the dining table. To notch it up a little bit, I switched off the lights and lit an aroma candle in the middle of the table.

She had cooked pasta and garlic bread for me. She did know what I loved to eat. Also, the next best thing happened after that was when I tasted it. So delicious, as if it has been served directly from God's own kitchen.

We were in the middle of dinner when she asked what had I been doing at Siddhant's place for the previous night. I told her that he guided me how to handle the complex times during a relationship.

She knew I was hiding something but she decided to change the topic soon after that. I just loved her for this, she believed in giving personal spaces to each other and believed that if something is meant to be shared, it will be.

She held my hand with both of her hands, kissed it and asked me to never break her trust. I promised that even if God came down to earth and asked me to leave her then I would have preferred leaving him then her as she was so perfect for me.

We then sat on the sofa and watched episodes of her favorite series F.R.I.E.N.D.S together. She questioned me if we would be like Monica and Chandler or like Rachel and Ross. These were the two couples in the series where the former was a fun loving couple who had no complications between them while the latter had walls of complication to break before ending up with each other.

I replied her in the sweetest words I could have thought of. I told her that I would be like a Ross who would love her Rachel till death but also at the same time would be funny like Chandler to her Monica. I wouldn't guarantee a life full of complications but at the same time would handle each complication in positive manner like Ross did.

'Do you know any real life Ross and Rachel in your real life' She asked while hugging me tightly like a teddy bear. I definitely had it in my mind but not on words. My lips were sealed and deep down under I prayed to God to unite them again.

'What are you thinking?' she asked while I was cuddling her.

'Nothing, just about a real life Ross and Rachel that I know. Just hoping that they end up being like Monica and Chandler.' I said with a hoarse voice.

'Do I know them?' she further asked.

'Definitely not the way I know' I replied.

She then came close to me; I could feel her warm breath on my lips. Her perfume drove me crazy, I cupped her cheeks by both hands, pulled her lips closer and then before she could realize what happened, my lips were already kissing her lips.

'I didn't see that coming' she said after we were done smooching.

'Well, I just proved that I can initiate a kiss too' I said while laughing.

The next morning, I woke up and Avni was sleeping right beside me. Sun was shining brightly right through the window directly to her face, making her face shining like a bright gold. I slid her hair to the back of her ear and got a sweet little smile in return.

I got up from bad, took a marker and wrote a quote on the bathroom mirror:

She slept like a sleeping beauty in her mansion

Making the world free of tension

She was actually a beauty

Which seemed to be her only duty

She was my soon to be wife

Whom I preferred calling my life

I got ready and tried to be as silent as I could. I was in my dressing room getting ready when she came in and handed me a tie to wear.

'Wear it, you'll look good in meeting today' she said with a blush.

'Sorry to wake you up, I tried to be as silent as I could' I said with my head hung low. She was looking so lovely and cute while sleeping that waking her up was the last thing that I wanted.

She tapped my head with her hand and said 'We work in same company Mr. Boss; I have my office too'

For a moment I forgot that she worked too, guess I had started to assume her as my wife.

I asked her to get her things by the end of the day.

We were about to take a next step in our relationship.

CHAPTER 14

The Funding

I reached office and went directly to my cabin. I opened my laptop and checked mails. Just when I was about to open the mail, I got a call from Siddhant for an important meeting.

I went to his cabin and he looked different than what he used to look before. He seemed to be in happy mood and had his headphones on. It was something he never used, rather I used to take it from his every time he ended up buying a new phone.

So when I saw him having his headphones on and humming something, I realized something was definitely wrong with this friend of mine.

'What is it, why are you so happy today?' I asked after seeing him.

'Why don't you think being happy is good. Anyway, thanks for hearing me out yesterday man. I had it under me since very long and I needed to get it out. Also, I am happy that the only friend whom I trusted the most was with me when I recited the entire life incident' He said.

His eyes told to whom this trustworthy friend was referred to, it was me.

By the way, how was your day with your girlfriend yesterday? Hope you enjoyed' He asked giving me the look that he knew that I was with her all the time yesterday.

But HOPE I ENJOYED?? I fucking lived every moment to fullest with her. In fact, I just couldn't tell how happy I was being with her. Most important thing about yesterday was I realized that she was the one who was actually made for me.

We soon jumped back to work and began discussing about industry trends and how we needed to change the company's image else in long run, it would somewhere or other would impact the company's performance in the market.

'How about if we fund or sponsor some NGO in their field assignment. It would definitely be good for public relations' Siddhant suggest. I wondered how he came to know about the fact that I was contacted by some NGO over the mail and I ignored that mail.

While I was about to say the next word, he burst into flames and asked me the reason of my ignorance to that mail. He said that I was already aware that we had to change people's mindset towards our company and I just added wood to fire.

As I was about to say the reason of my ignorance that I was busy sorting my life out with Avni, he asked if

I could arrange a meeting with them without further ado.

I loved this thing about Siddhant. He strictly kept professional and personal life aside. He knew that I was tired the other day but still as a strategic head, it was my responsibility to check important mails addressed to me.

Going outside, he said again that it wasn't important that how he got to know about the incident. Important was how me make it happen now.

On way back to the cabin, I met Avni in the corridor. She understood that I was in a bad mood and didn't spoke with me. She knew that I would have got angry at her for no reason whatsoever.

Back in my cabin, I searched the mail in my mailbox and after sometime I found that one mail among lakhs of other mails.

The mail was sent by *A. Juneja* who happened to be the founder of the NGO. The mail didn't have any clue as to whether the founder was a man or a lady. With high probability of being this unknown sender a man, I addressed him as *Mr Juneja.*

I wrote over the mail that we were ready to have a meeting with them face to face and review their proposal that they had for us. Also, I provided a preferred date and time just to avoid any confusion of date and place to meet.

I got the mail next day that they were fine with the date and time. I read till last and found that signature had a new addition to it.

It had now been changed to *Ms A. Juneja* with **Ms** written in black and bold. I forwarded that mail to Siddhant so that he could update his calendar accordingly.

In the mean while I searched about this NGO and found that it was headquartered in Haldwani, right from Siddhant's own city. I ran to him and informed about this. He was shocked and amazed. Shocked because he had no idea that a NGO is headquartered in his own native place working for the society. Amazed due to the fact that how a woman came forward to do charity and social work on her own. As far as I knew him, he had already made his decision to sponsor them irrespective of the amount of sponsorship that they required.

Further during my research, I found that this NGO was involved in woman empowerment which operated on business to business model. They manufactured raw material which was then used by other companies as to manufacture finished product. The entire workforce was made of woman, who worked in all departments beginning from production lines and ending up in back office finance department.

But nowhere on earth we knew or could find out who this mysterious *Ms. A Juneja* was.

Soon came the day when we had the meeting. A day before Siddhant, Avni and me discussed what we expected out of this campaign. Pitching Avni in this project was intentional since we were dealing with a woman founder this time and no one can understand a lady apart from a lady herself.

We asked Avni to coordinate with Ms Juneja regarding place of meeting and provide any help which she required. Avni and me waited for her in the meeting room when an office boy approached us informing that she was waiting at the reception.

Avni went with office boy to receive her and bring her in. I called up Siddhant confirming that she had arrived and meeting was about to start soon. Avni returned in few minutes with a lady who didn't seemed to run NGO or something. She seemed more of a model donned up in a pretty pink saree.

We shook our hands and exchanged cards. Instead of giving a single look to that card that she gave, I preferred looking at her. I had expected a lady in her early forties, carrying bundles of paper with her to tell us the benefits of sponsoring her NGO. However, she didn't seem to be a day older than twenty-five. Instead of bundles, there was a tablet which surely had a presentation that she prepared for us.

Her eyes were big which looked pretty in the kohl that she used. Her pink lipstick definitely went well with the saree she wore.

I asked her to sit while we waited for Siddhant to come. I don't think she heard me properly as she was still looking at the view that we had from our conference room. Well it was actually good. One could see entire city from that single room, giving clear view of nearby lakes, malls and highways.

I read the card which was still in my hand and my hands froze when I read the name on it. It read *Ms Shivyanka Juneja, Founder and Director.* The card fell from my hand and I stood still staring at her. Avni rushed to me and asked what had happened to me all of a sudden.

But before I could say her anything or ask Shivyanka anything, Siddhant walked in. As he walked in the conference room, Shivyanka stood right in front of him. It felt as if time had frozen for a moment.

Both of them were lost in each other's eyes, while I was lost in the card that had fallen from my hand on the floor still wondering, if that Shivyanka was actually here to meet us in the meeting. Avni struggled to understand what had happened to us.

In my mind, I recalled the entire story and connected the dots. Days before first separation in the childhood, they had promised with each other that they would follow their dreams. Shivyanka wanted to help the society by doing social welfare. She went to Singapore for studies after her college. What had been possible after that was Shivyanka came back from Singapore and entered into relationship with Rakul. She must have opened her NGO soon after returning and worked hard to make it what it was. Due to one reason or the other, she broke up with Rakul and ended up being alone.

Soon I was back in my senses when Siddhant shouted at her. He was angry because he believed to be Shivyanka's fault when she broke her engagement with Rakul. He ordered her to leave and called the guards to escort her back to the reception.

She had tears in her eyes and wanted a chance to speak, But Siddhant was already so angry that he listened to none, he banged the door of the conference room while going out and went straight to his cabin.

I ordered the guards to leave the conference room immediately leaving her back and gave her water to drink. Avni still struggled as she didn't know what had happened. I requested her to leave the room too. She didn't utter a word after that and left.

Shivyanka still sobbed after drinking the water. I went to her and apologized for Siddhant's behavior. She said that his anger was justified and she didn't take it to her heart. She felt bad because she didn't have any idea that he owned this company else she would have never approached us, also she never thought that she would be meeting her again under such complications.

She asked me to promise her that I would take care of him for her sake. I thought that this was the chance where I could get be their love angel and unite this Ross and Rachel back again. I promised her that I would get them back together.

She looked at me, her eyes were red and sought trust and confidence. I held her hands, rubbed them to make her feel warm. I told her that I would do anything that would be possible to get them back again.

She left with a positive note, with a confidence which I had to keep alive in her.

I went to my cabin with my head bursting in pain. I asked peon on the way to get me a painkiller. A lot was seen today and I just wasn't in a condition to bear any more surprises.

As I went in, I realized Avni was sitting on my chair waiting for me. Her face looked red in anger which seemed to have wait long enough for an answer.

Asking question as to what was keeping her angry was totally irrelevant because what she witnessed in the conference room was a big question in itself.

I made her sit down on the sofa which and gave her a water to drink. I decided to tell her the entire story but requested her not to judge anyone after hearing everything.

A story that kept me awake for twelve hours couldn't be narrated to anyone in an hour. It took me entire day to narrate the whole story. The story of friendship, promises, love and heartbreaks. A story where a blooming relationship was destroyed under the clouds of social status and class.

During the entire narration, her eyes remained wet and she reached out for tissues every now and then almost finishing the box that was changed in the morning. Later that day, she sat with me and discussed how the life had played unjustified games with them.

Life had given another chance to patch these love birds again. Avni and me spent an entire night figuring out what every alternative which could be get them back again. Every alternative had one or other hurdle to it.

After doing the analysis of every alternative available, it was decided that there couldn't be any set plan for it. All that we could thought of was keeping them together physically but for the hearts to be together, the wall of complications had to be broken down.

Time had complicated the things between them, so it was left to destiny to get back again. We could have just kept them together, but for the wall to break down, they would need to clear those misunderstandings.

CHAPTER 15

The Initiation

The plan began with Siddhant apologizing to Shivyanka. She was already informed about this part of the plan. For the things to start in normal phase, it was necessary that Siddhant felt comfortable around her and respected her.

Asking Siddhant to apologize to anyone was the toughest task. I went to his cabin the next day and told him that it would be bad for marketing if He any of the things came out in the market. I also further added that the title of capitalist would then be permanently ours if this sponsorship is pitched by someone else.

Hearing this, Siddhant got tensed. Nothing was bigger or important for him than companies image which included not even his own image. He asked me to call her back for the meeting and he would apologize to her. For the first time, I had to negate what he had asked me to do, I told him that she wanted him to apologize in her Delhi office. She had already been insulted in ours and she couldn't afford any more risks.

It initially included turning down the offer, but when informed that our rivals were in touch with here already, he immediately approved off it.

He asked me to take and appointment from her and he would apologize were her rude behavior the other day.

I called Shivyanka and informed what all happened during my discussion with him. She was so happy that she couldn't thank me enough.

The next day, Siddhant is reminded again for the meeting that he had with her. However, he couldn't be more ready had his company's image was not at stake. He made him so concerned about the incident that he believed it was the only chance which he had to save the image of the company. In my opinion it was definitely a last chance, but for relationship to work again.

He asked me to come along with him to give him company, but I decided to stay out of it. He headed to her office alone and returned back to the after spending few hours in her office.

'How was the meeting' I asked.

'Okay! I apologized and she is ready to come again for the meeting' he said.

Hearing this, I felt as if thousands of people danced inside my stomach celebrating the victory of step 1.

The second step involved calling her back to office.

I called her up again and said that Siddhant wanted to meet her for the meeting. Before, I could say anything further, she thanked me over the phone and also added that she couldn't be anymore lucky to have a friend like me helping them out.

However, I didn't let her hang up just by saying that. Avni and I were curious to know what had actually happened in her office.

She didn't tell it to us in the very first time, but however after insisting her again and again she blurted out some words.

She started off by saying that it was the toughest thing that we had achieved by asking him to say sorry.

She then told that Siddhant struggled to find her office. His navigation stopped working after some point of time making him stuck in the busy streets of Delhi.

He had to ask every person that crossed his path but none of them could help with the address. He then called her up and asked for directions.

She didn't tell it to him in the one go itself. She threw tantrums by canceling his calls frequently. After feeling pity for him, she picked his call and gave the directions to the office.

By the time he had reached office, his business suit was already drenched in sweat. Also, the air conditioner in her office didn't work adding more to his hurt ego.

He met her and apologized. She initially said to him that she would think about it as it was actually very half-hearted. She then further acted, by being on calls with one of her rivals confirming her funding proposals with them.

By the time the call was over, Siddhant was standing with her hands folded seeking forgiveness.

Her heart broke there itself and she requested him to stop embarrassing her. She confirmed that she would do funding with their company and would also help in improving the public image of his capitalist company.

She also added on the call that, she cried her hearts out when he left the office. Folding hands was the last thing she wanted him to do.

She then thanked Avni and me for helping her out in saving the relationship she once had with him.

After the call, Avni realized that it would had been better if these two were left alone for some time without any external influences, making this recovery a peaceful process.

Avni with the help of public relations department, drafted the action plan for the NGO in such a manner that Shivyanka and Siddhant had to do a field trip to some city to make it successful.

I loved the way she thought about saving the relationships and leaving them alone. Every passing day, she was again proving my decision to make her my life partner to be correct.

The next day, all four of us sat in the conference room discussing the action plan that Avni prepared. Both of them had their own opinions on it. Siddhant wanted to handle things from one place itself while Shivyanka wanted to explore various other places for better oppurtunities.

It was concluded that a field trip was to be done in the city of Haldwani, where the head-quarters of the

NGO was situated. Being from the city, would serve them with various strategic advantages leading it to be successful.

Convincing Siddhant was tough in this phase, but a word here and there on company's image did the job. Also, I convinced Siddhant to cut himself from any sort of communications with outside world during this campaign, as we didn't want competitors to get any hint that we were looking for ways to remove our capitalist titles therefore he had to leave his phone and laptop before departing for the city.

*****

The train was scheduled to leave next week at six in the morning from New Delhi Railway Station. Even at the end moment Siddhant didn't want to go. He was doing all of this to save his company's image. Avni and me came to station to give that last 'Bon Voyage' as a couple with complications and also to ensure that they leave for the city without fighting at the station.

The train was set to leave for the city which witnessed them growing up together, falling in love and then ending up by parting their ways for the betterment of their families.

Me and Avni reached back to our home at eight hoping everything to sort out between the two.

Days used to start with the prayers to God for sorting their differences out and nights used to end thinking it to be the worst plan of uniting these two.

Each and every day we checked our phones frequently hoping for a good news but got no success. Avni did had other contact details of Shivyanka but disturbing them was the last thing we wanted during this recovery process.

Avni and I got busy in managing the company in Siddhant's absence. By being in his shoes, I realized that it wasn't easy running a company of such large scale at such a young age. I guess this is what the power of love and promise is that they make people do the impossible tasks.

Four weeks had already passed and there was no sign of them. In the past four weeks Avni and I took our relationship to next step.

We arranged a meeting for our parents, to decide the fate of our relationship. Though we wanted to be together, but Avni didn't want to end up with me against her parent's will after all at the end of the day she was still an innocent Indian girl.

As expected, our parents were happy enough with the fact that we waited for their approval before getting married. They had no problems with our live in relationship too. In fact, my mom said that she couldn't think of any other girl better for me than Avni.

What if Shivyanka's and Siddhant's life was as simple as ours, had their parents allowed them to be together after completing graduation.

But then Siddhant would be working in some company at some managerial position than running one ad Shivyanka might have ended up being a house wife. It was the power of love that increased over a period of time when they were separated from each other.

One day the sun shone brightly and weather was pleasant, birds were chirping in the balcony giving me enough hints of what might had happened back in Haldwani.

Now all I had to wait was for the call or any other hint from their end which would end this mission with a successful outcome. I was doing my lunch when my prayers finally seemed to have been answered. I got a call from a new number on my cellphone and it was something what I had least expected.

'You are a stupid rascal! You know that I believe' said a voice which I longed to hear for past number of weeks.

'What is it now Sid, did you both end up fighting again' I asked acting innocent. I knew what it was about.

'You broke the promise that I made with myself, that I would never get back with Shivyanka' said Siddhant.

'What are you talking about man, I can't get a word that you are saying' I continued acting innocent. I knew what it was about.

'Shut up you bitch! Shivyanka told me everything and listen thanks, had you been not there I would have ended up being along' he said.

After hearing this, I was on the seventh sky. The day for which Avni and me had worked hard for had finally arrived. I kept him on hold, went to temple in my home and thanked God for listening to my prayers.

My voice over the phone while talking to him was so loud that Avni stopped all her work in kitchen and joined me on the dining table.

I kept the phone on speaker and connected portable charger to it. I knew it was going to be a long call because I wanted to know each and everything that happened back in the city.

I asked him to tell me word by word as to what all happened and how did they end up being together again. He said that sometimes one needs to work on the roots to improve things at the top.

They sorted their misunderstandings out and realized that there was no better for them than they themselves were for each other.

He then began narrating the happy part to his first not so happy love story

*****

CHAPTER 16

The Broken Engagement

I didn't interact with her at all in the train while she looked at me with a hope that I would talk in one way or the other with her. The passing trees and hills were my pass time in the train since I had no phone or laptop with me. After sometime I went outside my compartment to smoke near the washroom.

She followed me outside and asked if I remember the promise that we did with each other before separating from each other. I replied her in a rude manner that I didn't remember any promise I made with her back in school. In fact, talking to her was the biggest mistake of my life.

Hearing this, she began to cry. I didn't want that. I gave her my handkerchief, threw my cigarette in the dustbin and went back on my seat. She came back after washing her face. Her eyes were still red and sought forgiveness every time I looked at them.

I wanted to speak with her but my brother's broken engagement came in my mind whenever I thought of talking with her. I felt bad too myself. The moment I waited for where we could be together with each other forever in which no longer involved families was right there but still we had a new complication around us, the broken engagement.

I recalled what I got to hear from Rakul's mom that he was told by Shivyanka that she couldn't be with her since she loved someone else. Rakul felt cheated and had a major heartbreak. He was taken to psychiatrist to get his life back on track.

I didn't know the authenticity of any fact since I had not heard any of it from Rakul. We had been so busy in our lives that we hardly talked with each other now.

However, when her mom came to know about my business trip in the city, she invited me to her home for stay as all the hotels were full in the city due to summer vacations. Also, after my parents' death in an accident, I had place in the city to stay.

We reached Haldwani station at twelve in the afternoon. The sun was shining brightly over our heads, making it uncomfortable for us to stand. I was told by Rakul's mom that he would pick me up from the station. He was working in a startup which allowed him to work from home. It was then I asked her to leave for her home, as she was allergic to direct sunlight since childhood.

She was amazed and happy by the fact I still remembered it and I cared for her. I told her that it was just because it was hot and it wasn't good for health. It was then I saw Rakul coming, over the period of time he had changed a lot. He had smart hairstyle and fit body. He looked exactly what most models do in man's magazine. Girls would have actually killed each other to get married to him.

He ran as he saw me waiting for him and hugged me. He began crying as it had been a decade since he last saw me. I remember the last when I saw him was when I was leaving for Bangalore when I asked him to take care of Shivyanka for me. I wiped his tears away and then he saw Shivyanka beside me. There was an awkward formal handshake between the two.

She was about to leave, when Rakul asked that he would drop her on way. What I remembered was Rakul lived in opposite direction where she lived. I thought he wanted to spend time with her therefore he was dropping her home.

I sat on the back seat of his car, while Shivyanka sat in the front. The city changed a lot since the last time I was here. It was more of a time back then which was now transformed into a tech city. The houses were now smaller and Green Valley School was nowhere to be found. I asked for Rakul's phone and googled the school, it was found that school was burnt in a curfew. The lovely moments of childhood no longer existed. Not all changes are good after all.

However, I realized somethings still haven't changed when I saw Walkway mall and the park opposite to it. How could I forget my first date with Shivyanka? It was so perfect. I recalled what all I could of that first date: the dress she wore, the movie where I preferred looking her than the screen and the park where we gazed the stars.

Before I could realize, the car stopped in a society which resembled where I used to live in childhood before dad's promotion. The houses were small and the paint was faded. The cracks in the walls were clearly visible and the pollution from nearby factories covered the entire area. 'This doesn't look where you used to live. That was quite a nice place' I said. She said that her parents died in the beginning of this year in a plane crash. She had to sell that place off to clear of her father's debt and from then on she had been living here.

She told that she would collect me up next morning for her plant visit. I came on the front seat and Rakul now turned the car to his home's direction. 'So businessman doesn't carry their phones?' He asked. I told that I did it to focus on the project for which I was here for. He laughed and told that everyone knows Siddhant Shergill doesn't believe in charities and there was something which I was hiding.

Damn it! Even he had this capitalist mindset for my company. I felt that it needed to be changed soon. I changed the topic immediately and asked if he still went to psychiatrist. What he said next pissed and confused my mind.

He told that he never felt a need to go to a psychiatrist for anything, not even when her engagement broke. I told her that this was what her mother told me. He said that she spoilt Shivyanka's name in the society. We were to be blamed and not her. In fact, her family never said anything about us. Her mother basically brainwashed me.

Though it was true that she broke the engagement because she loved me instead of him. She agreed for engagement because of parental pressures to get married when she returned from Singapore. At that time, he was the only one who was with her. She couldn't think of anyone better other than him back then when no one had any signs of me, where I was and what I was doing. He supported her when she was alone and needed someone to share things with.

He never had any feelings for her after he realized that I loved her. He was just keeping the promise to compensate for tears which she shed by being in relationship with me.

The next day after the marriage she came to him to return back the ring. She said that she couldn't begin a new relationship which was based on the lie that she loved him. She loved me and would wait for me till I didn't return.

Hearing all of this, I broke down in the car. I cried loud enough making it embarrassing for him to drive. It got so embarrassing that he had to park the car at the corner of the road and console me up.

She always kept saying to everyone that she would wait for me every night right where we promised each other the most important promise of our life. He struggled to figure out which place was she referring to but I knew what was in her mind.

CHAPTER 17

Where It All Began

We went through busy lanes of the city until his home arrived. It was two already, and my body ache was killing me. I saw his mom at the entrance waiting for me. I touched his feet and showed fake respect because deep down under, she had lost the little respect I had for her after my mother died.

I took bath and had my lunch. I didn't want to stay a bit longer because the looks her mother gave me was killing me, especially after what Rakul told I wanted to run away from that place. I took Rakul outside the house and asked for his car keys.

He asked where was I heading to this time.

'You know it better I believe.' I said.

'Go get her brother!' he said and hugged me. His brotherly hug was what I was missing since childhood. A hug which felt complete in all aspects and had its own sense of support.

Over the period of Rakul had been from a stranger to a brother. I thanked him for being there with me whenever I required him.

'Now stop being emotional, got get your girl dude' he said.

I drove the car back to busy lanes, crossing her society. I stopped at a flower shop and collected a bouquet of blue orchids for her. I tried looking for a jewelry but I didn't pass through any on the entire route.

It was almost seven when I reached the park. Due to peak season time, the crowd had made the park congested. It was so congested that even if I tried I couldn't locate her there at that time. I moved from bench to bench, checked from people to people but I just couldn't find her.

It was nine at that time, I lost all hope and was heading my way back to the car parking.

'Are you leaving without even asking me how I was' said a familiar voice behind me. I turned back and saw her standing at a distance. She didn't look more beautiful the way she looked that day. She was wearing a blue jean with a simple white top and her hair were tied up in a pony.

'Did you kept your promise' I asked with tears in my eyes.

'I did, what about you' she began to shed tears too.

I ran up to her and wiped her tears with my fingers.

'Well I am one of the top businessman of the country' I said looking in her eyes.

'Where were you all this time. Are you now tired of troubling me?' she asked while laying her fingers in my hairs.

'I was working to fulfill my share of promise' I said while struggling to get down on my knees in order to propose her.

'You need not do that, yes I will marry you' she said with the cutest little smile which I saw in ages on her face.

*****

'Aww, what happened next?' I asked. By now Avni's and my eyes we filled with tears. We held our hands during this entire narration.

'Stop doing this aww thing, you know I hate it. What happened next is something private' he said while laughing.

It had been a long time I had seen him laughing like this.

'So did you guys do what you were actually supposed to do' I asked with concern. It had been on the news that Siddhant Shergill was nowhere to be found and it is believed that he might have fled away by giving his company in the hands of his consultant.

'Definitely! We covered all the rural areas which surrounded the city. We distributed sewing machines to the ladies and trained them on how to use it for generation of income. We are also in talks with the authorities now for setting a training center for these woman.' He said. His voice was full of pride and he was happy that at the end of the day, he did something for the society.

'By the way, I won't be returning back for quite a long time now. Shivyanka and me have to make up for the lost time' he further added.

'Be back soon, miss you buddy' I said as I hung up the phone.

Avni and I looked at each other with a sigh of relief. Things happened the way we planned it. Destiny played its game and settled them up together again.

The kids who studied together, now ended up together forever in a classroom of life. Where at every moment, life took their examinations of misunderstandings, broken trust and complicated relationships. Both of them handled every situation maturely and thus ending up topping the class of life.

*****